Radio Radio

Radio Radio

Graham Marks

BLOOMSBURY

First published in Great Britain in 2003 by
Bloomsbury Publishing Plc
38 Soho Square,London, W1D 3HB

A CIP catalogue record of this book is available from the
British Library

ISBN 0 7475 5939 2

10 9 8 7 6 5 4 3 2 1

Printed in Great Britain by Clays Ltd, St Ives plc

To Leo and the Boys Who Know Who They Are
A true inspiration, in more ways than one

Scene opens with an ESTABLISHING SHOT of a
bedroom. Hard to tell if it belongs to a
boy or a girl; there's stuff everywhere,
every flat surface is covered with
clothes, shoes, full ashtrays and empty
takeaway food cartons. The walls are a
patchwork of recent history, recorded in
Blu-Tacked music posters and club flyers.

CAMERA PANS ROUND THE ROOM, FOCUSING ON:

Music BLARING from a Sony mini-system set
up on the top of a cupboard and
surrounded by a collection of beer cans,
empty bottles and general crap; the MC is
ranting like a maniac about something,
his vocals just about in front of the
bass-heavy sample thundering away on a
seemingly endless loop. We can see that
the bedroom door is ajar. Suddenly, it's
SLAMMED SHUT by someone outside the room.

    STELLA'S MUM
Turn that bloody radio down, Stella!
How many times do I have to tell you,
girl?

CAMERA PANS TO:

Stella Whitely, standing by the bedroom
window, looking out. She turns towards
us, lighting a roll-up.

> STELLA
> (mutters to herself)
> A million times more than *you've*
> got the patience for.

Stella jabs a finger on to a button and
the sound dies. The room is quiet. The
radio is off. Camera ZOOMS in on Stella,
still standing by the window. She picks
up a cheap disposable lighter from the
window ledge and relights her roll-up.
Behind her, a phone starts ringing. She
picks her way over the untidy floor and
answers it...

> STELLA
> (sounding tired)
> Hi? Oh, hello Jase...yeah, I'm
> feeling fine now. (PAUSE) Been
> home since yesterday...yeah,
> everything seems cool...no, I'm
> glad you called.

Stella relights the roll-up.

STELLA
(brighter)
Where are you getting together...
the Cherrytree? When? OK, I can
make that, yeah...(PAUSE) Will
Jo...will she be — she will? No,
that's fine...(PAUSE) You did?
Last night? I'm sorry, Jason — are
you OK? Right, I'll, ah, I'll see
you there. Bye.

Stella puts down the phone and stubs out
the roll-up in an overflowing ashtray on
the floor. Sitting on the edge of her
unmade bed, she leans over to pick up
some flyers off the floor. We can see
they're advertising something called Reel
FM 103.5.
  The phone goes again and Stella lets
the flyers drop back on to the floor and
picks up.

STELLA
Yeah? (FACE BREAKS OUT INTO A BIG
SMILE) Nick! I'm good...I'm better —
you? That's great...they said there
was nothing they could get you on?
Fantastic!

Stella lies back on her bed.

9

CAMERA SHOT FROM ABOVE.

STELLA

What've your parents said? They
don't know? God, you're a jammy
bastard, Nick. (LAUGHS)...My Mum?
She's her usual self...yeah, she
rather had to know, didn't she...
the appointment? It's at 4.15 this
afternoon...You will? No, I'm not
surprised, I'm glad...It'd be
rough on my own. Yeah, he called
just now, told me about Jo...Yeah
...I'll meet you up at the caff.
Bye. Love you.

Stella sits up.

CUT TO FRONT SHOT OF HER LOOKING TO CAMERA.

Stella pulls up the sleeve on her left
arm to reveal a neatly wrapped and taped-
up bandage. She touches it lightly,
remembering. Then she stands and pulls
the sleeve back down as she looks round
the room.
   Going to her jam-packed closet, she
takes out a denim jacket, goes over to a
chair and picks up a black leather
shoulder bag. She EXITS, loudly shutting

the door.

   She's left the light on, and we hear
her clatter downstairs and slam the front
door, then:

    SHEILA WHITELY (O.S.)
   Have you remembered your
   appointment, Stella?

CAMERA ZOOMS IN ON THE FLYERS ON THE FLOOR, TURNING
ROUND TILL THE TOP ONE FILLS THE SCREEN WITH THE
MESSAGE:

REEL FM 103.5

UNDER YOUR SKIN

EVERY FRI/SAT/SUN

8 TILL LATE

ROLL:

RADIO RADIO TITLE SEQUENCE

Sequence runs over HAND-HELD LIVE FOOTAGE of
a club gig, mainly focused on an MC who's
on a small stage. He's standing in front
of a DJ and his deck set-up, rapping into
one half of a pair of studio headphones,
the curly wire hooked over his shoulder
and jacked into an amp in a stack to the
right of the DJ. The scene is lit by a
couple of MOBOS and the effect is very

strobe-like, with everyone's movements extremely jerky.

HARD CUT TO:

2 INT. CHERRYTREE CAFÉ — DAY   2

A group of six people are sitting round a table: Tom Cross is finishing off a plate of egg and chips, wiping the plate with a slice of white bread; CC Oweyo, Jo Knight and Jason Towne have empty plates in front of them and are drinking cans of Coke; sitting next to Sy Redstone, Stella Whitely is smoking a roll-up cigarette. The bell above the café door RINGS.

CAMERA PULLS BACK AND PANS OVER...

Nick Foster walks in, smiling broadly.

    NICK
  And a good morning to you all!

He pulls up a chair and sits next to Stella, taking the cigarette out of her hand and taking a drag. All the body language makes it obvious they are an item of some long standing.

TOM

Where've you been, Nicky boy — it's bloody two o'clock, mate!

NICK

That wanker Noddy gave me the late shift on Street FM again — two to four in the morning. And *then* he had the bloody nerve to say he couldn't afford my cab fare. I had to walk from Tottenham Hale.

CC

Those guys at Street are just ripping you off, man!

STELLA

But if he doesn't get on the air, how's he going to get better gigs, eh, CC? At least he's getting some time...you sounded great, babe.

NICK

How much did you hear?

STELLA

Fifteen minutes, tops...then I was out like a light.

CUT TO:

A shot of Jo looking at Stella, with a slight, almost imperceptible curl of the lip...

CUT TO:

NICK
You're right CC, I bloody *know* they're ripping me off...but the only way I can see of stopping that is by moving to a station that actually *wants* me, rather than being on one that uses me like slave labour.

TOM
(thoughtful)
Or...

NICK
Or what?

TOM
Or we start our own station and do it our way.

                 CC
          (singing)
          We did it owwwwwwww-r waaaaaaay!

                 NICK
          Riiiight...and how the hell are we
          gonna do that?

                 TOM
          If that idiot Noddy and his moron
          pals can do it, how difficult can
          it be? I reckon, between the six of
          us, we could do it.

CAMERA PANS ROUND THE TABLE.

Everyone's thinking about what Tom has
just said, but it's obvious that no one's
majorly keen. The CAMERA ends up back with:

                 TOM
          It's just a thought....(SHRUGS)
          better'n being ripped off, and it
          might be a bit of a laugh.

SFX: MOBILE PHONE RINGING.

CUT TO:

Jo, pulling her mobile out of her bag.

                    JO
     Shit! I'm late!

CUT TO NICK:

He picks up a ketchup bottle and goes
into rap.

                    NICK
     (singing)
     Making time, making time to make
     time, getting late, getting late,
     being outta line, it's all control,
     jus don think, do it my way, keep
     your head down, keep your mouth
     shut, you don't *have* a say...

Jo grabs her bag, chucking in her fags,
lighter and phone, and exits the café.

CUT TO:

Stella looking at Jo as she goes, cool,
then turning back to smile at Nick.

HARD CUT TO:

3   INT. JO'S KITCHEN — RADIO PLAYING — NIGHT   3

The rap that Nick started in the café is now playing on Jo's radio at home. She's in the kitchen, making a cup of tea and LISTENING.

QUICK CUTS TO:

4   VARIOUS INT.'S RADIOS PLAYING — NIGHT   4

As we switch from person to person — they're people we haven't met before, the audience for Street FM — the song progresses. Until...

HARD CUT TO:

5   INT. TRANSIT VAN — NIGHT   5

There are three people crammed into the back of a Transit. One is asleep, the second reading the sports pages of a tabloid newspaper; the third man has headphones on and is hunched over the bank of digital equipment that takes up most of the space in the van.
    We can just hear Nick's vocals and the music. Suddenly, the man with the headphones sits back and PUNCHES the air.

PHIL
(headphones)
Got the bastard!

MARTIN
(sports page)
About bloody time — give sleeping
beauty a kick and tell him to get
on the blower to Charlie...got an
address yet, Phil?

PHIL
Gimme a sec! (REACHES OVER AND
PRODS THE SLEEPING FIGURE)

BILLY
(sleeper)
Wha?!

MARTIN
Call Charlie; he's with Simmons
...we finally got a fix on that
poxy bunch who've been giving us
the runaround...Phil'll have the
address in a minute...tell him to
watch it when they go in, though, I
heard they had dogs.

      BILLY
Woof, woof! That'll be nice for
Charlie, he bloody *hates*
dogs...(PULLS OUT MOBILE PHONE AND
PUNCHES IN A NUMBER, LISTENS)
...Charlie?

HARD CUT TO:

6   INT. APARTMENT — SITTING ROOM — NIGHT   6

It's quiet and very low lit, furnished in
early Courts and MFI. There's no one in
the room, although you can just about
hear the sound of some muffled breathing.
Then a door opens and noise and light
spills out of what we can see is an
extremely heavily sound-proofed room full
of audio equipment — microphones, tape
decks, CD players...wires everywhere.
Nick walks into view.

      NICK
(over his shoulder)
See you tomorrow, Noddy.

A mobile phone rings somewhere in the
sitting room — its tone is the theme tune
from *The Sweeney*.

NICK
...Want me to get that?

Before Noddy has a chance to answer, the door to the apartment splinters apart under the assault of a steel battering ram. A bald-headed man with multiple earrings pokes his head out of the studio.

NODDY
(yells)
Genghis! Khan!

From the corner of the sitting room there's a hair-raising growl as two squat, incredibly powerful white blurs launch themselves across the short distance between the corner where they were asleep and what is left of the entrance to their territory.

NODDY
(orders)
Nuts, boys! NUTS!!

HARD CUT TO:

The scene is lit by the foggy glow of bad
street lighting and the flashing blue
lights of police cars and an ambulance.
The CAMERA pans round, passing curious
neighbours, kids and dogs until it finds
Nick. He's surrounded by Billy, Martin
and Phil.

ZOOM IN ON:

        MARTIN
What's your name again?

        NICK
Nick Foster.

        MARTIN
What were you doing there, Nick?

        NICK
Delivering...a friend of mine asked
me to drop some stuff off for a
friend of his.

        MARTIN
For the radio station?

                    NICK
I didn't know it was a radio
station...I thought it was just a
flat.

                    MARTIN
Just a flat? (LOOKS AT HIS WATCH)
Bit late for deliveries, isn't it?

                    NICK
(looking away)
Not really.

                    BILLY
What about the dogs?

                    NICK
What about the dogs? Everyone's got
dogs round here...in case someone
tries to break into their flat,
know what I mean?

Behind them the ambulance starts to move
off, its siren whooping.

                    MARTIN
Quit the clever stuff, lad, and
bugger off.

                    BILLY
               (surprised)
               Boss?

                    MARTIN
               Got nothing to hold him on,
               Billy...he was just there.

     Nick turns to walk away...

                    MARTIN
               (calls after him)
               I'd keep your nose clean from now
               on, though...Mr Simmons isn't going
               to look very kindly on anyone
               involved in tonight's little
               fracas. Know what *I* mean?

                    NICK
               Who's Mr Simmons?

                    BILLY
               The man in charge, (SMILES WRYLY)
               and one of the poor sods got their
               tackle tickled by those bloody
               dogs.

     FADE TO:

Nick and Stella are sitting on the floor amongst a mess of clothes, magazines, CDs and plates; Stella is dressed in a big, floppy T-shirt and smoking...the CAMERA pans between them and we see her digital clock's red LEDs flick to 5.37.

> STELLA
> Why'd you tell 'em your real name, Nick?

> NICK
> (tired)
> Didn't think...I was in a bit of a daze, tell the truth. One moment I was finishing my shift and about to come home, and the next all hell breaks loose...yelling, doors breaking down, Noddy going bloody *mental* and the dogs — you should've seen 'em, Stel!

> STELLA
> No thanks...

She gets up and walks over to her CD player.

STELLA
...Were the blokes hurt?

NICK
Ambulance job...had to be carried
out on a stretcher and stuff...
Noddy just yelled out 'NUTS!' and
that's what Genghis and Khan——

STELLA
(interrupts)
Genghis and Khan?

NICK
What can I say...Noddy's got a
thing about the Mongols...anyway,
the dogs got one of the guys who used
the battering ram thing on the door,
and this bloke called Mr Simmons who
turns out was the guy in charge. Blood
everywhere, very messy...grown men
crying...can't say I blame 'em either.

STELLA
(adjusting the volume)
But they let you off?

NICK

Had to, babe, no proof that I'd got
anything to do with anything...but
this DTI guy came on all official...

STELLA
(interrupts again, smiling)
That's what he is...official.

NICK
Whatever...Anyway, he kind of gave
me a warning, told me to keep my
nose clean.

STELLA
Clean of what? The station's closed
down, hasn't it?

NICK
They'll be up and running as soon
as they get a new rig fixed up and
sort out another studio...it won't
take 'em long, they've got wads of
cash behind them. Dunno where
from.

STELLA
You going back?

                    NICK
          Dunno...been thinking about what
          Tom said.

                    STELLA
          About what?

                    NICK
          About starting up our own station.

          Their conversation is interrupted by a
          rapping on the door of the bedroom and a
          MUFFLED voice from outside...

                    SHEILA WHITELY
          Turn that *bloody* racket down — have
          you got *any* idea what time it is?

                    STELLA
          How about getting our own place to
          live as well.

          FADE OUT.

9   INT. CHERRYTREE CAFÉ — DAY   9

     CLOSE IN ON:

     Nick, Stella, Tom and Jason sitting round
     a table drinking coffee.

STELLA

My bloody mum's driving me nuts.

NICK

She's OK.

STELLA

You don't have to live with her.

NICK

I do at least half *my* time nowadays, or so my mum told me last week.

TOM

Did you drag me down here to listen to you complaining about your mums? Cos if you did, I'm off.

NICK

Slow down...I wanted to talk to you about what you said, about starting our own radio station.

TOM

(mocking)
He listens! He doesn't just do the pointy thing (MIMICS AN MC ON STAGE) and shout!

NICK

Leave it out...look, d'you think we
could get a station together?
Could you, like, actually *build* a
rig and stuff? And where would we
put it all?

JASON

Slow down, Nick...we've actually
been talking about this...it's
possible, but it ain't easy, bruv.

NICK

Didn't think it would be...so, when
do we start?

JASON

Get real, Nick.

STELLA

That'd be a great name...

JASON

What would?

STELLA

Reel. R-E-E-L...we could call it
Reel FM.

                    JIMMY
              (gruff, heavily accented)
          Oi, you lot!

CAMERA PANS FAST TO THE BACK OF THE CAFÉ.

Jimmy, the Greek Cypriot owner of the
café, has come out of the kitchen, fag
clamped between his lips and wiping his
hands on a none-too-clean dishcloth.

                    JIMMY
          I don't rent office space, y'know,
          I sell coffee, tea an stuff to
          paying customers, innit...so unless
          you going to buy some more, it's time
          for you kids to piss off.

Jimmy turns and fiddles with a steamer
behind the counter.

CAMERA PANS BACK TO THE GROUP.

Nick, Stella, Tom and Jason all look at
each other. Nick shrugs, grins and gets
up.

                    NICK
          That's us told...(PAUSES) Reel
          FM...d'you know, I *really* like
          that...

          FADE OUT.
          CUT TO:

10 EXT. STREET — DAY   10

          A hand comes into view from the left-hand
          side of the screen and we see it SLAP a
          sticker on to a lamp-post and move on.
          The camera remains focused on the sticker
          long enough for us to read: *Reel FM 103.5
          — Under your skin every Fri/Sat/Sun 8
          till late*. Then it refocuses on the
          person walking down the street
          flyposting. The figure turns and looks
          over her shoulder...it's Jo.

          CAMERA PANS ACROSS THE STREET AND ZOOMS IN ON
          SOMEONE IN A DOORWAY.

          The person in the doorway is obviously
          watching Jo as she stickers the street.
          As she turns a corner, he drops his
          cigarette butt, grinds it out with his
          foot and sets off after her...

CUT TO:

11 INT. ROOM IN HOUSE — DAY   11

Three men are in a room. It's obvious
from the decoration that it's used as an
office for a company that works in some
guerrilla part of the music industry.
Shabby furniture. Walls covered with
posters. The two untidy desks strewn with
paperwork, full ashtrays and chipped
coffee cups. A cheap music system is
belting out a Jungle track.

One of the men — mid-20s, dressed in
jeans and a Nike sweatshirt — is pecking
away like a moronic chicken at the
keyboard of an old computer. Another —
30+, slacks and a Fred Perry top — is
playing on a GameBoy. The third — also
30+, dressed in a nice, sharp, silver-
grey suit — is standing, staring out of
the window. The CD sticks and goes into
one of those manic digital stutters. The
man playing the GameBoy slaps the machine
without even looking at it and the CD
jumps to the next track.

>   STEVIE
>   (computer)
>   Why'd you do that, Mel? That was
>   cool.

MEL
(*GameBoy*)
It was driving me nuts...just like
your bloody typing — tap, tap, tap —
it's like water bloody torture.

STEVIE
Oh, very funny...at least I'm doing
something useful, getting the
playlist sorted for Friday, rather
than spazzing on the GameBoy.
(IMITATES EXAGGERATED PLAY)

CHAZ
(suit)
Will you two shut it?

A mobile phone starts ringing.

CAMERA PANS OVER TO THE MAN BY THE WINDOW.

Chaz looks at the number before
answering.

CHAZ
Tyrone...what's up, man? (PAUSE)
Yeah, like I said, follow her, get
the address of where she ends up
and *then* ring me. OK? (CUTS
CONNECTION) He needs a bloody

diagram to get out of bed, that
boy.

STEVIE
What's he found out?

CHAZ
Nothing yet...but he's finally
spotted someone stickering for them
and was just 'checking in'.

MEL
Tyrone McRae, Private Investigator —
down the mean streets of North London
he must go!

CHAZ
True...watches far too much TV,
that boy. Anyway, (LIGHTS CIGARETTE)
shouldn't be long before we get a line
on who's behind this Reel FM...nip
'em in the bud before they get off the
ground...getting very crowded out
there...too many stations and we
can't control the message, and
Mr Sanders does like to control the
message...fucking DTI's getting
way too slack...

          MEL
     We just going to lean on them, or
     what, Chaz? (PUTS DOWN GAMEBOY,
     SITS FORWARD, INTERESTED)

          CHAZ
     The only things we're going to
     break is their rig and stuff...
     nothing physical just yet, Mel.

Mel sits back, chewing his nail and
looking thoroughly pissed off.

          STEVIE
     You never know, Mel, they may be
     really stupid and ignore the
     warning and then you'll have a
     chance to properly get angry.

          MEL
     I don't get fucking angry. I get
     fucking *even*.

Chaz's mobile goes off again.

CAMERA ZOOMS IN ON CHAZ AS HE ANSWERS THE PHONE.

          CHAZ
     ('Not-you-again' voice)
     Tyrone...

CUT TO:

12 EXT. STREET — DAY   12

Tyrone, walking slowly down a tree-lined
street, is talking on his mobile.

> TYRONE
> Yeah, she went into number 65, had
> a key, no knocking on the door or
> nothing. (PAUSE) Yeah, yeah, I
> waited and I saw her at a window on
> the first floor, with some bloke
> I've seen around. (PAUSE) There's
> nowhere to stay outta sight, Chaz,
> it's a street, man...(LOOKS AROUND
> AND GESTURES, AS IF CHAZ COULD SEE)...'K,
> 'K, don't lose it, I'll find somewhere
> to watch from...

CUT TO:

13 INT. HOUSE — DAY   13

Jo is standing with Jason near the window
of the first-floor room. She's standing
back, trying to stay out of sight of the
street, and indicating something to
Jason...

CAMERA MOVES TO JO'S POV AND WE SEE:

Tyrone walking down the street,
gesturing, as we've seen him do in the
previous scene.

CLOSE UP ON JO AND JASON.

> JO
> (worried)
> He followed me down the High
> Street, all the way from the
> Odeon...that's where I first
> realised, so God knows how long
> he'd been there.

> JASON
> (slightly annoyed)
> Why bring him straight here,
> Jo...couldn't you've rung me or
> something?

> JO
> Flat battery...and anyway, it's
> your dad's place, not where you
> *live*, Jase...look, he's stopped...
> he's hanging about — what're we
> gonna do? Who the hell is he?

37

JASON

Don't panic...it's not you he's
after, it's all of us...the radio
station. Nick called earlier, said
he'd heard someone was making
enquiries about us as soon as the
flyers and stickers went out. Bound
to happen, 'cos we've gone visible,
haven't we...(PICKS UP PHONE AND
DIALS AS HE SPEAKS) CC? Jase
...Look, Jo got followed by some
geezer when she was out stickering
...yeah, he's outside my dad's now...

CAMERA FOLLOWS JASON AS HE MOVES BACK TO LOOK OUT
OF THE WINDOW.

JASON

Yeah, still there...look, we're
gonna go out the back way and go to
Tom's, can you get over here now
and stake *him* out? Yeah, follow him
when he gets bored and pisses
off...Wearing? (PEERS OUT THE
WINDOW) Levis, Nikes and a grey,
hooded top, the usual...black kid,
six foot. (LOOKS AT JO FOR
CONFIRMATION. SHE SHRUGS 'SUPPOSE
SO') Yeah, (NODS) about that. 'K,
later.

        JO
   Why'd you call CC, where's Nick?

        JASON
   Said he was going to Tom's to 'help
   get the rig ready'...assistant
   screwdriver holder, more like!

CAMERA FOLLOWS JASON AS HE MOVES OUT OF THE ROOM,
JO GOING AFTER HIM.

Jason and Jo go downstairs and exit the
house into a small back garden.

        JASON
   We'll take the roundabout route,
   just in case your friend's got some
   back-up.

        JO
   (puzzled)
   Back-up?

        JASON
   Better safe than sorry.

CUT TO:

Jo, Tom and Stella are standing at the
bar of a dark, crowded club. Flashing
strobes light the place up, along with
the jaggedly edited video images playing
on one of the walls. No one's on the
small stage, but we can't quite see the
DJ who's working his decks behind a
scratched perspex screen.

CAMERA PANS AROUND THE CLUB.

We go from Jo, Tom, etc., past the DJ and
on to the entrance door, which opens and
lets in CC.
   He weaves his way across the packed
floor towards his friends. He shakes a
couple of hands, pats a few backs and
smiles a lot. CC is obviously a known
guy.

CAMERA ZOOMS IN ON CC AS HE ARRIVES AT THE BAR.

>   TOM
Where've you been...what happened?
You never called and your phone was
off.

>   CC
Later...somewhere quiet.

A voice rises above the track playing
and...

CAMERA CUTS TO:

The DJ — it's Jason — leaping up and down
and pointing at the stage...there are two
people up on the small stage: Nick,
looking relaxed and happy, and a very
cool Sy.

>JASON
>(excited)
>This is DJ Deep Groove telling you
>to listen up! Soon to be heard
>wreaking havoc on the Reel FM
>103.5 — it's MC D-Cee and Mr
>Standard MC!

CUT TO:

A lengthy scene — at least a minute,
possibly 90 seconds of screen time — made
up of quick cuts of the audience, with
close-ups of Tom, CC, Stella and Jo, as
well as feature shots of Jason, Sy and
Nick performing. Over everything is MC
D-Cee and Mr Standard MC's vocals.

MC D-CEE

'Money, glamma girls, cash...
Lick a tek, boydem come,
Then we make a dash!
'Cos it's DJ D, MC D-Cee
   alongside Mr Standard MC
Doing it how it should be
   Bubbly, Champagne, Hennessy, Brandy
Girls lookin' nice, girls lookin'
   sexy
Bashment affair, living lavishly,
Keeping it Reel on the frequency
   one oh three point five.
Keeping it live,
Don't MC for free
Need money to survive
And put credit on my cellie
When time we come, nuff party gone
And nuff jams soon run
Take a trip down wild west London
To link up with my bredrins in the
   corner of the city.
Next location, that's South London,
smash it like glass and move to the
   next one.
East side all the way up to North
   London...'

MR STANDARD MC

'It's me Standard MC...
I step inside the place and make
    the people lively.
Lay down the law, calm and correctly,
Till I switch like a blade and arms
    the party.
I don't really want to, but I know
    you'd do it to me.
So I'm staying on the top with D and
    D-Cee.
You, I, him and he make the crew
    jump like jiminy,
Right about now I'm drunk for Long
    Island ice tea,
I didn't come with no paper, I got
    in for free.
Why bring paper when they're paying me?
There's no cashback and no guarantee,
That's how I'm keeping it Standard MC.'

Playing out within this scene is the
continuing story of Jo and Stella's
relationship. We see Stella looking
adoringly at Nick as he performs. We see
Jason, in the relative calm behind the
decks, looking out at Jo. She's not

43

looking at him. Her eyes are flicking between Stella and Nick...

As the 60-90-second segment comes to an end, the camera PANS over the heaving crowd and ZOOMS in on a figure standing in the shadows, watching. A strobe flashes across, lighting the man's face up for a second as he drinks from a bottle of beer. It's Chaz.

CUT TO:

15 INT. OFFICE — NIGHT   15

Standard government open-plan office, mostly empty now because it's late but there's a corner where the lights are on. It's the DTI's Radiocommunications Agency. Three people are sitting round a desk: Billy, Martin and Phil, last seen during the raid on Street FM.

>   MARTIN
>   (tired)
>   Time to call it a day, boys...I've had
>   it. (RUBS FACE)

>   PHIL
>   Me too...don't you sometimes feel
>   we're fighting a losing battle?

Kind of a game where we shut 'em
down and no sooner than we have,
two more start up? I have bloody
nightmares about it.

BILLY
S'just a sodding job, Phil!

MARTIN
Now, now...remember what the good
Eddy Simmons, our glorious leader,
said only the other day, and I
quote—

BILLY
(interrupts in a pompous voice)
'This is not a job, it's a bloody
crusade!'...wanker...he'd make a
good traffic warden.

PHIL
Does take himself a bit seriously.

MARTIN
I know, but some of these toerags
(PICKS UP AND DROPS A HANDFUL OF
COLOURFUL FLYERS) don't give a toss
who they broadcast over...air
traffic control, hospitals,
emergency services.

45

                    BILLY
          Gets on my wick, that's all...comes
          on all the time like he's got a
          fucking rod up his arse.

     Billy gets up and searches in the pockets
     of the jacket he's hung on the back of
     his chair.

                    BILLY
          By the way, found this stuck to a
          lamp-post as I was coming on shift
          this afternoon.

     Billy reaches over the desk with a
     crumpled flyer and hands it to Martin...

     POV OVER MARTIN'S SHOULDER.

                    MARTIN
          Reel FM 103.5 (LOOKS AT HIS WATCH)
          ...what day is it? Thursday?
          No point in seeing if they're on
          the air yet...they're only doing
          the weekends. (GETS UP AND
          STRETCHES) Make a note, Phil...
          we'll keep an ear out for the
          buggers...

>   BILLY
> Look on the bright side, boss...
>   (PUTTING ON HIS JACKET) without
> 'em, we'd be out of a job.

CUT TO:

16 INT. CLUB — NIGHT   16

It's late, 3.00 a.m. kind of late. The
club is almost empty. The bar staff are
clearing up the mess left behind after
the night, and over in a corner, sitting
on a group of chairs and an old sofa, we
can see Nick, Jason, Sy, Jo, Tom, Stella
and CC.

>   SY
> What you guys looking so grim for?
> It was a *great* night.

>   NICK
> True, but I think we've ruffled
> some feathers out there...Jo was
> followed by some bloke today.

>   SY
>   (grins at Jo)
> She is a looker.

JASON
(frowning)
Listen, Sy...this is serious.

CC
...And I followed the geezer back
to Tottenham.

SY
Where'd he go?

CC
Some place called Violet
Productions.

NICK
Violent Productions, more like...
this is not good...even Noddy was a
bit careful around those guys...he
said a bloke called Chaz was the
front man, but you *really* had to
watch out for the one called Mick
or Tel or something.

CC
Whatever, but the guy I saw open
the door of the office — to let the
geezer I was following in. He was
here tonight.

                    SY
          Shit.

                    NICK
          Couldn'a put it better myself.

                    SY
          What d'you think they're gonna do?

          CUT TO:

17   INT. OFFICE — NIGHT   17

          We're back in the shabby offices of what
          we now know is Violet Productions.
          Everyone's there: Chaz, Stevie, Tyrone,
          and Mel, who's sniffing loudly and
          polishing a very nice carbon steel,
          rubber-grip claw hammer. You could cut
          the smoke-hazed atmosphere with a
          knife...

                    MEL
          ...bash their fucking heads in!

                    STEVIE
          This, in case you hadn't noticed,
          is not an episode of the fucking
          Sopranos! (TURNS) Will you tell
          him, Chaz?

                    CHAZ
              (ticked off)
         I'm just gonna tell the two of you
         to cut it out...I'm sick and tired
         of listening to you bickering. They
         haven't gone on the air yet, and we
         don't know where their studio is,
         so there's nowhere to go in mob-
         handed...even if we wanted to...

Chaz lights a cigarette, looking
pointedly at Mel, who sniffs and wipes
his nose on his sleeve.

                    CHAZ
         What we can do is have a nice,
         friendly little chat. I presume that's
         alright with everyone?

Stevie and Mel look at each other,
shuffling their feet and not looking at
Chaz...

                    CHAZ
         Great, glad we all agree...so,
         first thing tomorrow, I want you
         (POINTS TO TYRONE) back out on the
         street finding out where the rest
         of them live and where they hang
         out.

TYRONE
On me jacksie?

CHAZ
Don't be pathetic, Tyrone...and I
want you two to make sure it's all
sorted for the next gig. Mel, we
need more security...Mr Sanders
heard that Big Elliot knocked off
all the gear — the complete door,
all the blow, Jack and Jills, the
lot — at some massive party up in
Milton Keynes. Walked off with
bloody everything. Anyway, he also
heard that Big E might be planning
to have a go at one of ours.

MEL
He wouldn't dare!

CHAZ
Let's just be ready if he does, OK?

Chaz gets up and walks to the door.

CUT TO:

18 EXT. CLUB — NIGHT   18

Nick and Stella, arm in arm, walking
towards us down an alley to the street.

51

As they reach the street a door at the end of the alley opens and we see Jason, Jo, Sy, Tom and CC come out. CC and Tom are holding motorcycle helmets.

Nick looks back and waves as he and Stella disappear off screen.

CLOSE UP ON:

> SY
> Anyone coming down to Tony's for a cuppa and a bacon sandwich?

CAMERA PANS TO:

> JASON
> Don't you ever sleep?

> SY
> Not when it's dark!

CAMERA PANS TO:

> CC
> Think you're on your own on that one tonight, mate...big day tomorrow — we test run Tom's rig.

> TOM
> Power on! (DOES POWER RANGER STANCE, LAUGHING)

Tom and CC put on their helmets as he talks, and CC gets on and starts up a scooter that's been parked in the alley.

    SY
I'll listen out — alive on 103.5!

CAMERA ON TOM AND CC ROARING AWAY.

    JASON
(shakes head)
You couldn't pay me enough to get on the back of that thing...

Jason puts his arm around Jo, leaning forward to carry on talking to Sy.

    JASON
Tom must be completely mad, CC's made it his personal quest to see how far he can push the laws of physics.

THE CAMERA FOLLOWS THEM DOWN THE ALLEY, STOPPING AS THEY REACH THE STREET.

    SY
Sure about coming to Tony's?

                    JO
        Positive...we'll see you tomorrow,
        we're meeting at the Cherrytree
        round about fourish.

                    SY
        Later.

CAMERA PULLS BACK.

We see the trio split up, Jason and Jo
going one way, Sy the other.

FADE OUT.

19 EXT. STREET — DAY   19

        Shot at STREET LEVEL, we're looking across a
        reasonably busy suburban street at a row
        of shops.
          People are walking along the pavement,
        cars are criss-crossing the screen and
        for a second we see nothing that is
        relevant to the story.
          Then a scooter glides in from the left
        and stops, the rider pushing up the visor
        on his open-face helmet...

CUT TO FULL-FACE CLOSE-UP SHOT OF CC.

CC's parked and sitting on his scooter.
We can see the hands-free mic hanging
down by his mouth.

    CC
He's right outside now. Far
as I can make out, he's just
finished talking to someone
on his moby.

SWITCH POV TO BEHIND CC, LOOKING OVER HIS SHOULDER
DOWN THE ROAD.

We can now see Tyrone, on the other side
of the street, sitting on a garden wall.
He turns and stares up the road towards
CC.

    CC
No, I'll stay out here for now.
If I come in he'll clock me for
absolute sure and I don't *think* he
has so far.

In the distance, we see a car turn
sharply into the street from a side road,
wheels squealing. Tyrone looks away and
gets to his feet, shooting one last
glance at CC.

          CC
     Hold on, something's up.

CUT TO:

20 INT. CHERRYTREE CAFÉ — DAY   20

     Our POV is from behind the counter in the
     café, looking out towards the street. In
     the foreground we see Nick, Stella, Jo,
     Sy and Jason sitting round their
     favourite table; as well as the standard
     mess of coffee cups and ashtrays, there's
     also a small, slightly battered and
     taped-up radio-cassette player.
       Everyone, except Jason, is watching
     Nick, who's on the phone. Jason is
     looking over his shoulder, out of the
     window. Through the window we can see
     Tyrone standing up and pointing at the
     café.

          NICK
     What's up, CC...what's going on?

     We hear another squeal of brakes...

CAMERA PANS:

     ...and we see a car screech to a halt
     outside the café.

                    JASON
          I think we've got visitors...

We can see Chaz get out of the passenger
seat of a recent model silver Mondeo,
followed by Mel, who was driving.

CUT TO FULL-FACE CLOSE-UP SHOT OF NICK.

                    NICK
          Heads up, (ENDS CALL) CC says it's
          the guy he saw in the club last
          night...

The café's bell rings as the door opens
and Nick turns to look.

CUT TO:

21 INT. CHERRYTREE CAFÉ — DAY   21

At the sound of the bell, Jimmy has come
out of the kitchen, wiping his hands on
probably the same grimy tea towel.

CLOSE-UP ON:

         JIMMY
    (smiling)
    Afternoon, boys, what can I get
    you?

CUT TO:

         MEL
    (sniffs)
    Nothing. So fuck off and forget we
    was here.

In the silence that follows, no one
moves; we become aware that we can hear
the radio.

         CHAZ
    (to Jimmy)
    As it happens, sunshine, very good
    advice...go and de-grease something
    very greasy, there's a good chap.

Jimmy hesitates, thinks better of saying
anything, and exits.

POV SWITCHES TO THE SIDE; CHAZ AND MEL STANDING BY
THE DOOR.

         CHAZ
    (smiles insincerely)

So, the gang's all here. Nice.

   NICK
(frowns)
You looking for us?

   CHAZ
(hard, looking at Nick)
Listen, and listen good, because I
hate repeating myself. It would be
appreciated if you stopped what
you're doing with this Reel FM
shit. Right now, before there's a
chance of things turning nasty. OK?

   JO
Who'd 'appreciate' it?

   CHAZ
(still looking at Nick)
Never you mind. Now, have I made
myself clear?

Silence, except for the music on the
radio, which fades out and we hear Tom's
voice name-checking Reel FM...
   Jo looks at the radio, then quickly up
at Nick; Nick looks at her, then glances
at Chaz and Mel as he reaches to turn it
off.

CUT TO CLOSE-UP OF:

> CHAZ
> Now *that* is really bad timing,
> wouldn't you say, Mel?

CAMERA PANS TO:

> MEL
> Fucking terrible, Chaz.

Mel steps forward, reaches across the
table and hits the radio-cassette player
with a hammer he's had concealed behind
his back.

> MEL
> Oops.

> CHAZ
> Clumsy boy.

> JO
> You can't do that!

> CHAZ
> I think you'll find we can, love.

Chaz turns, looking at each person round
the table, one after the other. Then he
nods to Mel to go.

CHAZ
It's been a pleasure. Cheerio.

As the door closes behind Chaz and Mel,
Jimmy comes back out of the kitchen.

JIMMY
(almost hysterical)
What the fuck is going on — this a
café...I'm gonna call the fucking
police!

(O.S. — SFX: more squealing tyres as Mel
and Chaz drive off.

JIMMY
(yelling)
Get their fucking number plate!

NICK
Calm down, Jimmy...nothing happened
to your café...no need for the
cops.

JIMMY
(amazed)
Nothing happen? Some bastard walk in
and tells me to fuck off and clean

something greasy and then smashes my
table with a hammer? You call that
nothing?

    JASON
(angry)
He trashed *our* radio, Jimmy. *Your*
table and chairs are fine!

    STELLA
Calm down, Jason, it was just an
old car boot thing...

    JASON
That's not the point!

Jo glares at Stella in a 'how dare you!'
kind of way and is about to speak when
the door bell rings and breaks the
moment. Everyone looks up or turns.

CAMERA PANS TO THE DOOR.

    JIMMY
(hysterical again, pointing)
Is another one!

    CC
(puzzled)

Another what? (TAKES OFF HIS
HELMET, LOOKS AT THE TRASHED RADIO)
I see they left their calling
card...what happened?

JIMMY
What happen? (STABS HIS OWN CHEST WITH
INDEX FINGER) I nearly had a fucking
heart attack is what happen!

NICK
We got well and truly told to back
off and forget Reel FM, is what
really went down.

CC
And smashing the radio — what was
that all about?

JO
We had it on, listening to the test
broadcast. Just after the guy in
the suit had told us to lay off,
everything went quiet — and Tom
came on with a name check. That's
when the other one trashed it with
a hammer.

CC
Well, (SHRUGS AND RAISES EYEBROWS)
at least we know the rig works.

CUT TO:

22 INT. OFFICE — DAY   22

The DTI's Radiocommunications Agency is
buzzing. Martin is at his desk sorting
through a mound of paperwork as Phil comes
in, tucking a pencil behind his ear...

PHIL
Just had a call from Johnny...he's
been doing a trawl up around the
Palace and picked up something on
103.5...a test broadcast, apparently.

MARTIN
(sits back)
What are they calling themselves?
Reel FM? (PHIL NODS) Did Johnny get
a location?

PHIL
(shakes head)
Off the air too quick, boss.

MARTIN
They'll be back...

Tom's room. It's more of a workshop with
sleeping facilities; the bed's up on a
raised platform, leaving the floor area
free for work benches, two ragged office
chairs, a plan chest, a couple of old
easy chairs and a small coffee table with
a dope plant growing in an old, blue,
Chinese pot. Tom, CC, Nick and Jason are
present. Tom is concentrating on rolling
a home-grown joint.

CAMERA ON:

    JASON
Bloody great, isn't it? We start
and finish on the same sodding day!

CUT TO:

    CC
Who's said anything about
finishing?

BACK TO:

    JASON
That bloke looked like he didn't
care *what* he hit with his hammer...
are you like, *anxious* to find out

what it feels like to have a
fractured skull?

      NICK   JASON
(pensive)   (nonplussed)
Mel.   What?

      NICK
That's the name I couldn't
remember...the wacko Noddy was
talking about, the one with the
hammer, his name's Mel. And in the
suit is Chaz, like Noddy said.
Interesting, isn't it?

      JASON
(frowns)
What are you on about, Nick?

      NICK
We know almost as much about them
as they do about us...who they are,
where they operate from.

      JASON
So? You gonna go round there and
break *their* radio?

Nick sits back in the easy chair, smiling
to himself. Jason looks over at CC, who
shrugs. Silence. Then the sound of a

66

Zippo being fired up...

CAMERA PULLS BACK AND PANS ACROSS TO TOM, LIGHTING
THE JOINT.

> TOM
> (smiling)
> Shall we just chill for a minute?

Tom makes a big deal of taking a hit off
the joint, and then passes it on.

> TOM
> As I see it, our main problem —
> apart from the Violent Brothers
> (BREATHES OUT) — is, now that we've
> got ourselves a working rig, where
> the hell are we going to put it?
> And Nick's right about our knowing
> quite a bit about them.

> JASON
> Why?

> TOM
> Knowledge is power — didn't you
> learn *anything* in history?

> JASON   CC
> I didn't do history.   Children.

67

NICK

OK, truce everyone (HANDS JOINT
BACK TO TOM AND GETS UP)...Jason's
got a point, we have a big problem
with the Violets. Tom's right,
we've now got to find somewhere to
put the rig — *and* somewhere safe
for the studio — and CC's right,
we've been acting like children.
But it was fucking scary in the
Cherrytree...

TOM
(very relaxed)
R-i-g-h-t...(SITS UP, LOOKS ROUND
THE ROOM) where are the girls?

CC
Sy took 'em up West in his car —
they were going to see about
getting some T-shirts done.

TOM
(excited)
We're having T-shirts?

NICK

That's the plan...
Anyway, anybody
got any ideas about
the rig and the
studio?

TOM

What colour?

JASON

God, you reached the
Silly Zone quick
today. (TAKES SPLIFF,
TAKES A DRAG AND
DOGS IT)

TOM

Hey!

NICK

Tom, this is serious...if we don't
find a secure home for Reel FM, all
the sweat will've been a total
waste.

CC

Sod the sweat, think of all the
money.

NICK

Let's not...my parents're gonna go
doolally when they find out what
I've done with that money I got.

        CC
(pretending to hold a microphone)
What's it feel like to be a major
investor in a brand new business
venture, Mr Foster?

        NICK
(getting into character)
From the heart of my bottom, I'd
just like to take this opportunity
to say a big 'Thank you' to all my
fellow investors — they may not
have had the pennies, but they made
up for it with pounds of their
precious time!

Tom is watching this performance,
giggling; Jason obviously wants to get
matters back on track.

        JASON
Why d'you think the Violent
Brothers are interested in us
anyway...what kinda trouble can *we*
cause them — they do raves, don't
they?

        CC
Think about it, Jase...what are
most pirates on the air for?

They're owned by the promoters
...they *promote* the parties.
They're sure as hell not doing it
'cos they love the music.

    JASON
And?

    NICK
And we'd be additional noise...a
distraction they could do without,
not part of their gang. That about
right, CC?

    CC
On the button. I'm not saying we've
bitten off more than we can chew,
but Violet are a bunch of very bad
boys.

    JASON
Telling me.

    NICK
Exactly how bad?

CLOSE-UP ON:

    CC
My next up brother, the one works

for my dad? Asked him to do a bit
of checking up for me...there's
this place, Companies House, where
you can find out loads of info,
accounts, directors, shareholders,
other companies they own...the
whole family tree thing. And he
also ran the name by a mate
of his on the local rag.

     NICK
I just know I'm not going to like
this...what'd he say?

     CC
Violet's down as being in business
to 'promote musical events',
according to something called their
Memorandum and Articles of
Association, whatever the hell that
is. But they're part of a much bigger
group called Sanders Entertainment
Services.

CAMERA PULLS BACK TO INCLUDE:

     NICK
Never heard of them.

CC

They do gig security, transport,
sound and lights...at least, that's
part of what they do.

JASON

And what's the other part?

CC
(careless)
Oh, you know, drugs, money
laundering, fencing, shylocking.
North London's finest, I'm told.

CC gets up, walks over to the work bench
and picks up a screwdriver.

CC

And the two people we've met are
Charles 'Chaz' Morton — the suit —
and Melvin James, the nutter with
the hammer. Used to be known as 'Ten
Pound', apparently.

NICK

How'd you find *that* out?

CC

It's what the bloke on the paper

told my bro. Got the name from the
kind of hammer he liked to use.

   NICK
Didn't *really* need to know that.

   CC
Apparently he's changed to
something he can carry around
more easily.

   NICK
As we found out.

   TOM
(to himself)
I reckon black T-shirts with a
white logo...that'd look the
business!

   JASON
Ignore him and he might go away...
So, what're you saying — this has
got out of hand and we better give
up now before someone gets hurt?

   CC
I'm saying we've got to be *very*
careful — partly 'cos what we're
doing isn't *entirely* legal, as

we're all aware, but mostly 'cos
these guys obviously don't pussy
about...But I think we've come too
far to back out now, and tomorrow,
we should go house hunting...

CUT TO:

24 EXT. STREET — DAY   24

30-second sequence, with loud music
track, of the different sets of friends —
Nick and Stella on foot and bus; CC and
Tom on the scooter, Sy, Jason and Jo in
the car — on street corners looking at
local papers, on the mobile, looking in
newsagents' windows, obviously
searching...

CUT TO:

25 INT. FAST FOOD OUTLET — DAY   25

Six exhausted people. Stella, Nick, Tom
and Jason are at a table, Jo and CC are
queueing. You can tell by the body
language and facial expressions that this
has not been one of their most successful
days. Enthusiasm has not overcome market
forces.

CAMERA ON:

> STELLA

Whoever thought we were just gonna
walk out and find a place, you know
(SNAPS FINGERS) like that, must've
been on something.

CAMERA PULLS BACK.

> TOM

We had shared a very splendid Casa
Mia spliff...

> STELLA

(turns to Nick)
That explains a lot...so what are
we gonna do?

> NICK

Kick back and take stock...where's
Sy?

> STELLA

Parking his car somewhere vaguely
legal.

> NICK

We're running out of time, we're
running out of money, it's cost us

all a shedload to get this far, and
it looks like we've hit a brick
wall.

CC and Jo appear, each carrying a tray
loaded with plastic boxes, paper-wrapped
burgers, fries, shakes and Cokes.

> CC
> Who's for a chicken meal, regular
> fries and a diet Coke?

> JO
> Double burger, no pickle, big fries,
> chocolate milk shake?

CAMERA FOLLOWS AS FOOD, DRINK, SERVIETTES ETC. ARE
HANDED OUT.

> NICK
> (takes a plastic container)
> Thanks, Jo...I'll take Sy's as well,
> he had the same as me.

> JASON
> (sits back)
> No time, no money and no place to
> go. Looks like we're buggered then.

          STELLA
     (annoyed)
     Why're you always so negative?

          JO
     (sharply)
     Leave him alone — why are you
     always picking on him?

In the embarrassed silence, Stella sits
back staring at her chips. Jo opens up
her burger and takes out the pickle.

          JO
     (tense)
     I specifically asked for *no* pickle —
     you heard me, didn't you CC?

CAMERA CUTS TO:

Sy slipping into the seat next to Nick
before CC has time to answer.

          SY
     (smiling)
     Wanna hear the good news or the bad
     news?

          CC
     Good news, before someone slashes
     their wrists...

SY
Have I missed something?

CC
Later...

NICK
What's up? Found a free parking
meter, but it's only got five
minutes left on the clock?

SY
No. My mum just called on the moby —
my Gran's gone into the nursing
home...remember I told you she was
going a bit ga-ga, Nick?

Nick, stuffing a burger in his face,
nods.

STELLA
(slightly shocked)
How come that's the good news?

SY
I get to move into her flat...on
the 25th floor of a block on the
Highfields Estate!

                    STELLA
          You sick bastard!

                    JASON
          What's the bad news?

                    SY
          (mock sad)
          The rent's only paid for the next
          three months!

          Sy gets pelted with chips.

          CUT TO:

26   EXT. CAR — DAY   26

          We're in Sy's car as he's driving Jo back
          home...

                    JO
          Thanks for giving me a lift, I
          really didn't want to go on to the pub
          with them.

                    SY
          S'OK, I was going this way to my
          mum's...(PAUSE)...What did I miss
          back there?

JO
Back where?

SY
C'mon, girl, let it out...I know
there's something between you and
Stella...gotta be a fool not to've
picked *that* up. Except I'm new
round here, so I don't know what
it's all about...maybe talking to
someone who hasn't a clue what's
going on'll help.

Jo sits looking out of the passenger-side
window, resolutely not saying anything.
Then she gets a cigarette pack out of her
bag.

JO
D'you mind if I smoke?

SY
Burst into flames, for all I care,
just tell me what the fuck's going
on between you two.

JO
(emotional, near to tears)
It, um...it used to be me and Nick,
you know? For ages...

SY
He dump you for Stella, that it?

JO
No...nothing like that...nothing so
bloody simple...

Jo takes ages to get her cigarette lit,
delaying tactics to keep from getting to
the nub of the problem. We can see that
she's deeply affected.

SY
You don't have to—

JO
(interrupts)
I've got to tell someone...(LIGHTS
FAG, STARING STRAIGHT AHEAD) I feel
like I'll explode if I don't,
really lose it big time...I've been
holding this back for years...since
it happened...no one knows, not
even Nick.

SY
(nervous)
Knows what, Jo?

82

JO

I got pregnant (TURNS TO LOOK AT
SY) Can you stop the car...I think
I'm going to throw up.

Sy looks round, indicates and pulls over.
Almost before the car has stopped Jo has
opened the door and been sick in the
gutter.

CUT TO:

27 INT. PUB — DAY   27

Jo and Sy are sitting at a corner table.
Jo, smoking a cigarette, has a glass of
water in front of her and Sy is sipping
at a half pint of lager.

JO

It was Nick's...there'd been no one
else.

SY
You said he didn't know?

JO
We'd talked — you know, once we'd
started sleeping together — like,
about babies and stuff. Nick was

so...so *positive*...a baby would
ruin everything, all his plans, he
said...he was, *we* were so
careful.

SY
Accidents happen...I've had a
couple of close calls myself.

JO
Yeah, but it's OK for you blokes,
you aren't the ones who get the
kid. Anyway, after I'd missed my
period by a week I, you know, did a
test...and it was positive.

SY
You didn't tell him?

JO
Why...what would've been the point?
I already knew how he felt. So I,
um...(VOICE GOES SMALL) I got rid
of it.

SY
How the hell d'you do *that* without
anyone finding out? I mean, what
about your parents?

JO

It's amazing what you can do when
you're really desperate, Sy...and I
was *desperate* not to lose Nick.

Jo stops talking, just sits and fiddles
with one of the rings she's wearing.

JO
(not looking at Sy)
I went to the Marie Stopes...they
asked me if I was sure I wanted to
terminate, and told 'em I was...it
took less than two hours one
afternoon and when I got home I...I
pretended to have a bad case of
food poisoning and stayed in bed
for a couple of days.

A single tear runs down her cheek.

JO
(turns to look at Sy again)
It was easy...I felt shitty, so
didn't even have to act.

SY
(quiet)
Jesus...how old were you?

JO
Seventeen.

SY
So, where'd it all go wrong...I
mean, no baby, no problem, right?

JO
(tired)
What a fucking fairy tale *that*
turned out to be...it was as if
Nick knew something had happened
because everything changed between
us...I tried to be the same, but
there was this huge thing, this
gulf...it was the baby, not being
able to talk about it, not being
able to grieve or cry or anything...

As Jo is talking more tears start to run
down her face...Sy reaches over and takes
her hand. She grips it tightly with both
of hers.

JO
(swallows hard)
...we ended up having this
screaming row. It was horrible, the
things we said to each other...but
I still didn't tell him about the

baby. And that was it, we split
up...and I didn't have a baby *or*
Nick any more.

    SY
(points to her glass)
Shall I get you something stronger
than that?

    JO
(nods and smiles weakly)
Vodka Red Bull, thanks.

Jo lights another cigarette and, as she
waits for Sy to come back from the bar,
checks her face in a small mirror she
gets out of her bag.

    SY
(concerned)
You OK?

    JO
Yeah (TAKES A DRINK) thanks...Sorry
for dumping on you, but once I'd
started talking, you know, it was
like a dam bursting...I couldn't
stop.

SY

My mum always says it's better out
than in. (MIMICS WEST INDIAN WOMAN'S
VOICE) 'Better out than in, Simon,
that's what I halways say, if you
aks me!'

Jo can't help but be amused by Sy's
performance.

SY
(more serious)
...so you and Stella, you just
don't like the girl 'cos she's with
Nick, right? Not that she's bad or
nothing?

JO
No, she's not bad; and yes, I hate
her because she's with Nick...and
yes, that's not her fault, not his
fault either, I suppose.

SY
(quiet)
You still love him, don't you?

JO
(voice breaking again)
Yeah.

SY

And you're with Jason 'cos he's
Nick's best friend, and that means
you can still be around him?

JO

(pulling herself together)
Pathetic, isn't it? (STUBS OUT
CIGARETTE, FORCEFULLY) I really
should get a life.

SY

You really should tell Nick what
went down, girl, is what you should
really do.

JO

(pensive)
Is life always so black and white
for blokes? (GETS UP) Come on,
you've got to go and see your mum
(LIGHTS CIGARETTE)...Are we starting to
clear your Gran's flat tomorrow?

CAMERA FOLLOWS THEM AS THEY WALK TOWARDS THE DOOR.

SY

Yeah. (HOLDS PUB DOOR OPEN) You
smoke too much, you know that?

Jo rolls her eyes as she walks out of the pub. Sy follows after her and the door closes behind them...

CUT TO:

28 INT. GRAN'S FLAT — DAY   28

Organised chaos...we are in a flat that, from the decor and furniture, etc., was the home of an old lady. There are big cardboard boxes everywhere, some full, some being filled and some being moved out.

CAMERA ON:

          TOM
     What is it about old ladies and
     their net curtains? We're twenty-five
     floors up, the nearest block is a
     couple of hundred metres away and
     these things could stop a bullet,
     let alone stop people seeing in!

          NICK
     They're staying...good security.

Sy walks back into the flat, dusting himself off, followed by Jason.

CAMERA PULLS BACK:

    SY
I can get one more box in, then
I'll have to do another run to the
charity shop.

    NICK
They must think it's Christmas!

    JASON
If they see one more box of
assorted tea towels they're gonna
tell us to fuck off back where we
came from.

Stella comes into the room. She's
carrying an armload of carefully ironed
decorative tea towels.

    STELLA
If I see another load of assorted
tea towels — she must have the
world's largest collection, Sy.

    SY
(shrugs)
My mum hoards toilet rolls...you
know, in case there's a world

shortage? Anyway, give us a box and
we'll get going.

    JASON
Where's CC? He got a sick note from
the doctor saying he can't lift
anything, or what?

    NICK
(as he packs a box)
Called in earlier...said something
about having to check up on some
stuff and he'd be round later to help.

    JASON
What stuff?

    NICK
God knows...but I *bet* it's got
something to do with the info his
brother gave him.

CLOSE-UP ON:

    STELLA
Hope he's being careful.

CUT TO:

Shot CUTS IN to a close-up of CC's face,
helmet on, hands-free mic visible; the
only facial movements are his eyes
flicking from side to side. He's on his
scooter, moving fast through the traffic.

CAMERA pulls back and we see him riding
down a street we haven't seen before. He
does a double-take and swerves to his
left — across the path of the car behind
him — and squeezes in between two parked
cars. The guy he's cut up beeps him as he
goes past, angrily flicking him a V-sign.

The CAMERA stays on CC as he gets a
battered *A to Z* out from under his seat
and makes as if he's consulting it. The
CAMERA closes in on him and we can see that
he's actually spending more time looking
at what's in front of him than at the
pages.

Our POV now changes so that we can see
what CC is looking at. It's a well-kept,
three-storey Georgian building with a
sign by the front door. Three large
initial letters read 'S.E.S', underneath
which is spelled out 'Sanders
Entertainment Services Ltd'.

CC turns his back on the building and
looks at his watch as he chews his lip —

knowing he should be helping at the flat
but wanting to stay where he is. He
doesn't see Tyrone walk into view, going
towards the front door.

Tyrone's about to ring the doorbell
when something makes him look over at CC.
We see him look away, ring the bell,
frown, think, look back and then raise
his eyebrows. He's remembered where he's
seen CC before! He pushes the door open
and disappears inside.

CUT BACK TO CLOSE-UP OF:

CC
(holding mic to his mouth)
Nick Foster...(WAITS FOR THE NUMBER
TO RING)...D-Cee ma'man! Yeah I'll
be there soon, just had to check out a
thing or two...(TURNS BACK TOWARDS THE
HOUSE) I'll tell you — oh shit...

THE CAMERA DOES A QUICK PAN BACK ROUND TO THE
HOUSE.

CC's eyes widen as he sees the door of
the house has opened and Mel has
appeared.

94

CAMERA CUTS TO CC JUMPING ON HIS SCOOTER AND
STARTING IT UP.

        CC
    Catch you later, man!

There's a QUICK CUT to Mel as he starts
running towards CC, halting at the kerb
as a stream of traffic stops him from
crossing. We can see he's very
frustrated. We can also just see — most
of it's hidden up his sleeve — his
beloved hammer.

CUT BACK TO:

CC as he takes his chances and darts into
his lane, causing a car to hit the
brakes.
    POV changes to show CC coming down the
street towards us, grinning, obviously
thinking he's got away with it by the
skin of his teeth. Then, behind him,
flying out of a tiny mews, comes another
scooter.
    Its two-stroke engine is screaming like
a banshee, tyres squealing as the rider
does a skid turn right in front of a car.
More horns and the sound of a breaking
tail light as the car is rear-ended.

CC glances over his shoulder at the
noise, and his expression changes as he
mouths 'Fuck!' and twists the accelerator
grip back as hard as he can.

CUT TO A C/U SHOT OF MEL, SHOUTING:

        MEL
    Get the bastard, Tyrone!

CUT TO:

30 EXT. STREET — DAY   30

This is the start of a 45-second chase
sequence that pits CC, who we know is a
mad dog on his scooter, against Tyrone.
And Tyrone, it turns out, is no slouch
either...
    This will be real riding (a bit like
Bullit on scooters), with plenty of
wheelies and other astonishing two-wheel
tricks, as CC tries everything he knows
to lose Tyrone. But Tyrone is sticking to
him like shit to a blanket.
    At one point Tyrone manages to get
level and tries to kick and punch CC, but
he suddenly reduces speed so that he's
now behind Tyrone. He then makes a very

tight left turn and he seems to have done
it.

But Tyrone finesses his way back into
the chase, until CC pulls one last
desperate rabbit out of the hat — a trick
which leaves him on the road and his
scooter badly scraped, but Tyrone in the
Grand Union Canal.

CUT TO:

31 INT. GRAN'S FLAT — EARLY EVENING   31

In all the flat now looks quite
different. Most of the granny stuff has
been moved out, the furniture has been
rearranged and each piece has colourful
throws on it. There's a lava lamp, a few
posters on one of the walls and someone
has draped a shawl over the central light
hanging from the ceiling.

Jo is tending to CC's wounds — a very
bad case of road rash on his left
shoulder, arm and hip — as Nick, Tom,
Jason and Sy listen to what he's saying.

Stella comes out of the kitchen with a
cup of instant coffee and puts it down on
the low table next to CC.

CAMERA ON:

                JO
    Sorry, but this is gonna hurt,
    CC.

                CC
    Can't hurt much more than it
    already does. (JO DABS ON SOME
    ANTISEPTIC) Ow! Jesus!

                JO
    Sorry, sorry, sorry!

PULL BACK TO INCLUDE:

                NICK
    What the *hell* were you doing there
    anyway?

                CC
    I was following the trail back...I
    wanted to see what we're up
    against.

                JASON
    We *know* what we're up against —
    bloody nutters with hammers...did
    anyone follow you back here?

CUT TO:

Jo shooting a look at Stella, who looks away to...

    CC
Hardly, Jase...what with the
bloke's scooter being at the bottom
of the canal.

CUT TO:

Jo glancing at Sy — a look we can see is
caught by Jason.

CAMERA PULLS BACK TO:

    NICK
Wasn't the brightest move, bruv.

    CC
How was I to know they'd be there?
Sod's bloody law, that was.

    NICK
Doesn't matter...nothing broken,
eh?...(PAUSE)...what d'you think of
the place?

CC picks up coffee, winces with pain, as
he sips and looks around.

                CC
(smiles)
Nice...wonder what Grannie would
say if she could see it now...

                SY
(gets up)
Wanna guided tour? (HELPS CC TO HIS
FEET) This place is just about
perfect.

                TOM
(bubbling)
We got complete line-of-sight to
the next block (GOES TO FRENCH
WINDOWS AND POINTS OUT) which means
I can fix up a microwave link on
the balcony and the rig isn't even
on this building...

                CC
Slow down, Tom — microwave?

                NICK
Tech speak...you don't wanna know.

                SY
Kitchen (POINTS AS HE WALKS), clean
enough to eat off the bloody floor,
but not likely to stay that way for

long...bathroom, main bedroom and
presenting...the Reel FM studio!

CAMERA FOLLOWS SY AS HE WALKS INTO A TINY 2ND
BEDROOM.

    SY
Doesn't look like much, but we're
moving the decks and everything in
tomorrow...

    NICK
I reckon we'll be up and running by
next weekend!

    SY
And talk about sod's law —
Saturday's when Violet've got their
next big event...I picked this up
earlier on (TAKES A FLYER OUT OF
HIS BACK POCKET, UNFOLDS IT AND
READS)...Concrete 6x6 — 12 solid
hours of non-stop music, blah,
blah, blah...Look at all the bloody
sponsors they've got, *and* it's a
tenner to get in...they must be
raking it...

SFX: MOBILE PHONE RINGING IN BACKGROUND.

STELLA (O.S.)
Jase! It's your mobile!

CUT TO:

32 INT. GRAN'S FLAT — EVENING   32

Sy, Tom, Nick and Stella are sitting
round in the low-lit main room. The
atmosphere is the complete opposite of
the last scene...Stella's sitting on the
edge of an armchair holding a mobile...

CAMERA ON:

NICK
What did he say?

STELLA
His dad's place was trashed...
whoever it was had just bust the
front door in and torn the place
apart.

NICK
I don't think we have to look very
far to find who did it, Stel...that
was where they followed Jo back to,
remember? This is their way of
getting their own back for what CC
did...

                STELLA
         (mutters)
         Stupid cow.

                NICK
         What?

                STELLA
         (angry)
         Well she is...and you ignore it 'cos
         she's your old girlfriend, everyone
         knows it!

Nick frowns, completely puzzled and looks
round at Sy and Tom for some kind of
support or explanation. They both stay
silent, Sy making a hands-up-palms-out
'Nothing to do with me, mate' gesture.

                NICK
         I don't know *what* you're on about,
         Stel...I don't ignore anything, and
         Jo...(EXASPERATED SIGH)...we've
         been over this before...she hasn't
         been my girlfriend for bloody
         ages...what're you losing it
         for?

                    STELLA
       I'm not fucking losing it...why
       don't you stand up for me when she
       has a go? And you *know* she's only
       with that poor sod Jason so's
       she can be around you as much as
       possible, right?

Stella looks at Tom, who shrugs,
embarrassed, and then at Sy, who stares
straight back at her.

                    STELLA
       What?

                    SY
       (calm)
       I think you guys should do this in
       private, without an audience.

                    STELLA
       (edgy)
       Oh you do, do you?

                    SY
       (solid)
       Yeah, I do, as it happens. Nick?

Nick gets up and holds out a hand to
Stella. She hesitates, then takes it and

they leave the flat together, watched by
Sy and Tom.

>   SY
>   Women...

>   TOM
>   What was that all about?

>   SY
>   I think it's called the eternal
>   triangle, mate...and someone always
>   ends up getting hurt...

CUT TO:

33 INT. STELLA'S BEDROOM — NIGHT   33

No lights are on and the only
illumination comes from the moon and
street lights. We can see Nick is naked
from the waist up and sitting up in the
bed, leaning back against the wall, but
no facial expressions are visible. He has
one arm loosely round Stella, who's
snuggled up to him, fast asleep. Her face
is in what light there is and we can see
that her mascara has run.
   Nick reaches to his left, picks up a
cigarette and lights it. In the butane

flare we can see his face is very thoughtful. Carefully, he gets out of bed without waking Stella, going to stand by the window...

CUT TO:

34 INT. GRAN'S FLAT — EVENING   34

We're in the kitchen and we can tell that a few days have passed as it's in a right state. No way could you eat off the floor now. Sy is boiling a kettle as Nick puts instant coffee into some mugs. They're both dressed completely in black.

CAMERA ON:

     SY
Everything cool?

     NICK
(over his shoulder)
Totally straight...meant to say sorry for the other night, but—

     SY
That's OK, man, but I was meaning about the antenna on the roof of the other block? (HANDS THE KETTLE

106

TO NICK) D'you think I'm right
about where to put the rig and
stuff?

                NICK
        (makes the coffees)
Yeah...I mean, you've been up there
and scoped it out — how'd you
manage to not have to smash the
lock to get on the roof?

                SY
Easy. Someone had already done a
number on the door and the
council'd repaired the damage with
a cheap padlock...I've got a friend
works in a hardware store, I told
him the make and he showed me how
to open the lock with a paper clip.

                NICK
You can do that?

                SY
On my word. Then I took the lock
down and he got me a proper key.

Sy takes a key ring out of his pocket and
holds it up by one particular key,
smiling.

                 SY
        So, we about ready to go?

                 NICK
        Let's go and check with the
        Technical Director, shall we?

        He picks up the coffee cups and they both
        exit the kitchen.

        CUT TO:

35 INT. GRAN'S FLAT — EVENING   35

        The main room looks like the HQ for an
        SAS raid. Sy, Jason and Nick are dressed
        all in black and standing around looking
        nervous. On the table in front of them is
        a grey metal box, about the size of a
        large encyclopedia volume, with a number
        of different colour wires coming out of
        it.
          Next to it is a fairly large coil of
        thickish cable, a couple of serious
        torches and various tools. On the floor
        are three black holdalls.

                 TOM
        (nervous/excited)
        D'you want to go over everything

                        108

one more time? (CHECKS WATCH) Nick,
you've got the wiring diagram? You
remember what I said about earthing
the rig...

NICK
(interrupts)
We're cool, Tom...we've been over
this so often we could do it
blindfolded.

TOM
Can't be too careful...so, the code
is?

JASON
(as if by rote)
Two long flashes, followed by two
short flashes, when everything's in
place and powered up.

SY
Then you switch on the microwave
gizmo (JERKS A THUMB OVER TOWARDS
THE BALCONY) and send a test
broadcast.

NICK
And send back three short flashes
if everything's roses, two if it
isn't...

                    SY
          (confused)
          Can someone explain to me why we don't
          just call each other on the mobile?
          I can get with the programme when
          it comes to wearing black and
          stuff, but why the flashing of the
          lights? Where's that come from?

Nick begins to speak, frowns, then stops
and looks at Jason and Tom.

               NICK
          You're right...why aren't we using
          our mobiles, Tom?

               TOM
          (embarrassed)
          Seemed more, um, realistic.

               NICK
          Realistic?

               TOM
          (resigned)
          Call me on the phone...

CUT TO:

Nick, Sy and Jason, plus their bags, are
in a crappy municipal lift, grinding
their way up to the top of the block of
flats where they're going to install the
rig and antenna. The lift's fluorescent
lights flicker erratically, the steel
walls are covered in intense graffiti and
you can almost smell the piss.

> JASON
> This is disgusting.

> NICK
> Makes you really appreciate the
> joys of living at home.

> SY
> Oi! I live in one of these places
> now!

There's a screeching noise; the lights
stutter and buzz and the lift judders to
a halt. The lights go out.

> JASON
> Oh, for God's sake!

SY
(turning on his torch)
Hang on, don't panic.

JASON
I'm not panicking.

NICK
Some bastards have ripped the
emergency phone out.

Nick holds a length of curly wire into
the torch light. It should have a phone
on the end of it, but doesn't.

SY
Silly sods probably live here and
all...(SHINES TORCH AT CONTROL PANEL)
...anyone remember what floor
we'd just passed?

JASON
Think it was the 17th or 18th,
something like that.

Sy carefully presses the button for the
19th floor. Nothing happens. He presses
again, harder. Still nothing...

                    SY
          Fuck! (SLAMS THE PANEL WITH THE
          PALM OF HIS HAND)

The lights flicker back on and the lift
jolts into action for 3-4 seconds...

                    SY
          Who needs an engineering degree?

...only to wheeze to a halt again. This
time the lights stay on.

                    SY
          (shakes his head)
          One step forward, (JABS AT THE 19
          BUTTON AGAIN) two fucking steps...

There's a squealing noise and the doors
open to reveal a dull, grey-blue
corridor. The three friends don't need
any prompting to get out.

                    SY
          ...forward. Let's get outta here!

37 INT. STAIRWELL — NIGHT   37

The boys are doggedly climbing the
emergency stairs to the top of the block;

Sy's in front, followed by Nick, then Jason. Lit by sickly yellow lamps above each flight's emergency exit door — some of which are busted — the stairs are a filthy and depressing place to be.

POV LOOKING DOWN THE STAIRS TOWARDS SY.

    SY
Me, I'm walking the whole way back down, man...every step.

    NICK
Watch where you tread, Sy...it's a junky's paradise up here.

    JASON
Let's hope we don't *meet* any of them.

Sy looks back over his shoulder at Nick, who grins back at him and raises one eyebrow. We see Jason is checking behind him, down the stairwell, as Sy turns back and looks upwards...

    SY
We're nearly there, guys...

CUT TO:

38 EXT. ROOF — NIGHT 38

We're outside, looking at a weatherbeaten
door. We can hear scuffling noises, a
loud click...and the door opens inwards,
letting the sick yellow light from the
stairwell spill out on to the roof.

CAMERA ON:

Sy coming out, putting his bag down and
looking round to orient himself.

> SY
> (whispers)
> The water tank's over there, (JERKS
> THUMB RIGHT) that's the vent shaft
> over there, (NODS LEFT) the louvred
> window thingy isn't locked...I'll
> come and give you a hand as soon as
> I've got the antenna fixed.

Sy shoulders his bag, waves and lopes off
into the night. Jason and Nick look at
each other...

> NICK
> Now or never time.

CUT TO:

39 INT. GRAN'S FLAT — NIGHT   39

The lights are off in the main room, but
on down the hall in the 'studio'. Tom's
sitting in the relative darkness by the
open French windows, looking out at the
block opposite through a pair of
binoculars. There's a muffled ringing and
we see him fumbling in his jacket pocket,
finally bringing out a mobile. He answers
it still looking through the binoculars.

    TOM
(distracted)
Yeah? Oh, hi Mum...(PAUSE)...I'm at
Sy's...he's a friend of mine...no,
you haven't met him, he's an MC,
like Nick...they work together...
(SUDDENLY SITS FORWARD) *Yes*! They
did it!
  Nothing, Mum, just something on
TV...look, I'll see you tomorrow,
Mum...(STANDS UP) No, I'm not
trying to get rid of you but I'm
expecting a phone call...OK, OK, I
am trying to get rid of you but
only because I'm expecting a call!
Yeah, an important one. (SIGHS,

116

EXASPERATED) No not from a
girl...tomorrow, yeah. Bye...

Tom cuts the phone connection and puts it
down, still looking through the
binoculars.

TOM
(almost under his breath)
Well done, Sy...*exactly* the right
place!

CUT TO:

40 EXT. ROOF — NIGHT   40

We see Sy on top of a vast water tank,
one hand steadying the antenna he's put
together, the other holding a cordless
electric drill as he drives home the
final screw. He waggles the antenna and,
satisfied with his handiwork, stuffs his
tools back in the holdall, snaps off the
torch and climbs back down to the roof.
Waving in the direction of where he
knows Tom is, he runs over to the vent
shaft where Nick and Jason are.
Access to the vent is through a louvred
'window' some 5 metres up the tower. Some
rusty iron rungs are set into the

117

brickwork beneath. Bag slung over his shoulders, Sy climbs his way up to the open window.

CUT TO:

41 EXT. VENT SHAFT — NIGHT   41

Inside the vent tower, which is about 2 metres square, Jason and Nick are standing side by side on a narrow ledge. Jason is hammering a plug into a hole he's just drilled, while Nick shines a torch on the area where Jason is working.

CAMERA ON:

Sy's head and shoulders appear in the window.

> SY
> How's it going, guys?

> NICK
> (mocking)
> Super, absolutely *super*, old chap...(WIPES SWEAT OFF HIS FOREHEAD, LEAVING A GRIMY MARK) It's cramped, hot and one false move'd send one of us plummeting ...(NODS

DOWNWARDS) We also broke a drill bit
and I dropped a bolt through the
fan blades...otherwise it's great,
we're almost there — how about you?

JASON
(tetchy)
Keep the *sodding*
torch steady,
Nick...

SY
All done...
want me to do
the juice?

NICK
What are you waiting for?

CUT TO:

42 INT. GRAN'S FLAT — NIGHT   42

Same as before — Tom sitting in the semi-
darkness staring out of the French
windows through the binoculars. Then the
door buzzer goes and he hurries over to
answer it.

TOM
Who is it?

JO (O.S.)
(muffled)
Me, Jo.

Tom opens the door to let her in.

JO
Why're you sitting in the dark?

TOM
(gestures with binoculars)
Makes it easier to see what's
happening.

JO
(excited)
What *is* happening? (GESTURES FOR
TOM TO GIVE HER THE BINOCULARS)

TOM
Nothing...I could see Sy putting up
the antenna, but he's gone to help
the others, inside the vent tower.

Tom's mobile phone rings. And he grabs it
out of his pocket and fumbles it on...

TOM
Nick? (NODS TO JO) Am I ready? I've
been ready since you left...shall I
run the tape? Two seconds!

JO
Can I say hi?

TOM
No time. (ENDS CALL) Come and give
me a hand.

Tom runs over to the French windows and
out on to the balcony. He looks back and
points down to a cassette player on the
floor. It's next to a radio.

TOM
(calm, in charge)
Press *play* on the cassette when I
tell you to, *then* switch the radio
on...I've already tuned it to
103.5...

Jo nods and waits, watching as Tom checks
the wires running from the microwave
radio link.

TOM
Now!

Jo pushes down the *play* button and we see
the tape begin to move. She then reaches

over and switches on the radio and we see
the digital LED display leap into life
showing the bright red frequency 103.5...

For a second nothing happens. Silence.
Static. Then the speakers burst into life
— it's a tape of Sy and Nick performing,
the same tune we saw them do at the club.

> JO
> You *did* it! (HUGS AN EMBARRASSED TOM)

> TOM
> (amazed, grinning)
> Not bad for a doper (NODS HIS HEAD)...
> Christ, nearly forgot, better
> ring 'em to say it's all working
> and they can get off the roof!

> JO
> This is *so* great!

> TOM
> Doesn't get much better.

CUT TO:

43 INT. VENUE — DAY   43

We're in a huge club, situated in a large
Victorian warehouse. All the windows have

been blacked out so, even though it's early afternoon, all the lights are turned up. What looks reasonably classy and funky under strobes and glitterballs at night just looks tatty and cheap in the unforgiving glare.

Bar staff are clearing up, and in one corner Mel is holding court. He's sitting back in a booth, a drink on the table in front of him.

Standing looking at him are a dozen or so men with no necks, all wearing tight T-shirts and well-defined muscle groups. All are over six foot, seven are black and all of them look hard as nails. Not bright, but very hard.

CAMERA ON:

    MEL
...the rules here are no different to anywhere else you've probably worked, right? *Everyone* gets checked at the door — handbags, pat downs...but do *not* get over enthusiastic with girls who aren't wearing enough to hide what they were born with. (SMILES) It only gets their boyfriends all wound up. Oh yeah, and no drugs.

          KEV
(frowns)
None at all?

          MEL
Don't be stupid, Kev...of course
there's gear, but only what the
house supplies, right? And those of
you not on the doors, keep an eye
out for any freelances. Is that
clear? Kev?

Kev, standing straighter, hands gripped
behind his back, flexing his muscles,
nods. Behind him the main door into the
big room opens and...

CUT TO:

Chaz walking in with a trim, older man of
55-60. He has grey, thinning hair, very
well groomed, and is wearing a sober but
sharply cut suit and highly polished
penny loafers. The image is only slightly
let down by the large diamond solitaire
ring and very flashy Cartier watch he's
wearing.
    You can tell by the way he walks the
man is used to being in control, and,
unusually, we can see there's a slight

nervousness about Chaz. The man stops and looks round the room, wrinkling his nose at the stale booze and smoke smell.

> MR SANDERS
> (wipes his nose with a
> brilliantly white handkerchief)
> This place stinks...can't you open
> a window?

> CHAZ
> Ground floor, Mr Sanders...they're
> locked for security purposes.

> MR SANDERS
> Right, right...(LOOKS OVER TO WHERE
> MEL IS)...are they the new boys?

Chaz nods that they are.

> MR SANDERS
> I'm sure Mel's doing his usual
> superb job of bringing them up to
> speed on how we do things, but a
> word from the boss can't go amiss —
> am I right?

> CHAZ
> On the nose, Mr Sanders...(SMILES)
> always works for me...

They walk over to where Mel's sitting.
Mel stops lounging around like he owns
the place as soon as he realises that the
man who does is coming his way.

> MR SANDERS
> (slightly sarcastic)
> Nice to see you hard at work, Ten
> Pound...these fellers know what
> they're doing?

The circle of men look round to see who's
talking and, realising he's important,
break to give him direct access to Mel.

> MEL
> (slightly nervous)
> Just running through everything one
> more time, Mr Sanders.

> MR SANDERS
> Mind if I have a word?

Mel silently indicates that it would be
completely fine if Mr Sanders did
whatever he liked.

> MR SANDERS
> You may have been unlucky enough to
> have come across a scumbag called

Elliot Williams...a *fat* bastard who
also goes by the name Big Elliot,
or Big E.

As Mr Sanders eyeballs each of the men,
we get a good look at them. They nod, and
you can tell they know who Mr Sanders is.

    MR SANDERS
He's not only a fat bastard, he's a
lazy fat bastard who likes money
but doesn't want to work for it...
He prefers to take it off other
people who *have* worked. People like
us.
  Now, he normally operates north of
the M25, but word is, he's getting
greedy and wants to come to town.
Word is, he likes the look of *us*,
thinks we're a soft target. And I'm
telling you boys now, I am not
having it...you have my full
permission to be not very nice to
anyone trying it on in this club,
OK?

The men all nod, including Mel, who
realises what he's doing and stops. Mr
Sanders turns round to look at Chaz...

MR SANDERS
You coming for a spot of lunch,
Chaz?

CHAZ
Very kind of you, Mr Sanders...

CUT TO:

44 INT. CAR IN STREET — DAY   44

We're looking through the windscreen of a
fairly new Vauxhall Vectra with three men
in it. Two men are sitting up front — one
white, the other black — and there's one
white guy in the back.
The man in the back is quite large. If
you weren't being very nice, you'd call
him a fat bastard.

CAMERA ON:

FRANK
(driver)
Eyes right! Looks like they're
leaving, E.

BIG ELLIOT
(rear passenger)
Ponce! Look at him lording it up

with his chauffeur-driven Beemer
and flunkies.

CUT TO:

Shot from the Vauxhall, we see Mr Sanders
and Chaz coming out of the warehouse and
getting into a black BMW. Above the
entrance is a large fluorescent sign
announcing that this is a club called
Concrete. As the car drives away we...

CUT BACK TO:

    BIG ELLIOT
Have you boys seen enough? I know I
have.

    DENNIS
(front passenger)
Everything cool, boss. They flash,
we gonna get their cash!

    FRANK
You still think Saturday's the best
night to hit them?

    BIG ELLIOT
Know what, Frank? I do.

                    FRANK
          (starting the engine)
          Saturday it is, E.

     CUT TO:

45   EXT. ESTATE — DAY   45

          We join Sy, Nick and Jason walking down
          the street, deep in conversation. Sy and
          Nick have backpacks, Jason is carrying a
          fully loaded record bag.

                    NICK
          We've got another (CHECKS WATCH)
          three hours before we go on the
          air...is there anything we've
          forgotten before we go up?

                    JASON
          (pats record bag)
          This is the last of the vinyl...and
          I took the tapes up this morning.

                    SY
          Nick and I've got the beers, and
          the girls said they'd be bringing
          some food.

      NICK
(gets out his mobile)
D'you think we should bell up to CC
before we start the Long March?

      SY   JASON
Nah...and you never   On the other
know, the lifts might   hand...
be working.

They turn a corner and we see the
entrance to a block called Meadowbank.

      NICK
Who'd have thought you'd get fit
running a radio station?

CUT TO:

46 INT. GRAN'S FLAT — THE STUDIO — NIGHT   46

The small second bedroom appears even
smaller because it's now full of
equipment, some very basic mattress and
foam rubber sound-proofing and its window
is blacked out.
   Jason is sitting on a ratty old office
chair, headphones on, decks lined up and
a microphone — gaffer-taped to the
business end of an Anglepoise lamp that

no longer has a lamp — which is inches from his mouth.

Sitting in the corner, on another piece of skip rescue furniture, Nick is quietly smoking a fag. On his lap is an expensive-looking Shure microphone.

Standing in the doorway, CC is looking at his watch and then back down the hallway.

> CC
> Tom! Everything OK down there?
> (PAUSES, THEN GIVES A THUMBS UP)
> Right, Jase, it's a five, four, three, two, one — GO!

As CC closes the door, Jason pulls the mic towards him, flicks a couple of switches, lifts a needle ready to put it on to a record.

> JASON
> (looking over at Nick)
> This is Reel FM 103.5 on the frequency that is alive!

Jason lets the needle down and brings up the fader.

CUT TO:

47 INT. GRAN'S FLAT — MAIN ROOM — NIGHT   47

Tom, Jo, Sy and Stella are gathered round
the radio, and we can see CC running down
the corridor to be with them. We can see
the LED display showing the 103.5
frequency and the speakers are blasting
out the track Jason has just put on.

    SY
Historic, fucking historic!

Cutting in on top of the track, we hear
Jason name-checking himself.

    DJ DEEP GROOVE
This is DJ Deep Groove on Reel
FM 103.5 — call your shouts in on
the Reel Line — 076 1249 2349,
that's 076 1249 2349 and taking
over the groove is MC D-Cee...

CUT TO:

48 INT. GRAN'S FLAT — THE STUDIO — NIGHT   48

Jason cues up another record and signals
to Nick that he's on.

MC D-CEE
Right about now we're live on
   your FM dial.
And for the meanwhile
Make all those screwface break
   a smile.
Hundred per cent well versatile,
Making money by the pile,
Agile — and you know we've got
   style
In time, when I drop my rhyme,
sit down steady on the bass line,
Ring the bell, flip the dime,
2 by 2 we rise and climb.
What's yours is yours and
   mine is mine,
And this sound here is not a
   crime.

CUT BACK TO:

49 INT. GRAN'S FLAT — MAIN ROOM — NIGHT   49

Nick's voice comes through, loud and
clear, and everyone leaps up, cheering.

CUT TO:

SHOT FROM ABOVE: SY, JO, TOM AND STELLA ARM IN ARM,
DANCING ROUND IN A CIRCLE.

134

CUT TO:

50 INT. VENUE — NIGHT   50

We're at Concrete and, now that it's night,
it looks right. Up on the first floor
things are beginning to cook; the place
isn't packed yet, but it's well on the way.

CAMERA ON:

                    DJ
        ...and tomorrow night, when you're
        chillin', tune into a brand new
        station I hear is up on the
        airwaves tonight — I'm talkin Reel
        FM 103.5, check it out, check it
        out!

CUT TO:

In the middle of the crowd we can see
Mel. Overhead, the CAMERA follows him as he
pushes his way through the dancers. He's
looking like he could bite the head off a
baby...
    The CAMERA stays on him as he makes his
way towards the DJ, but before he gets
there, Stevie pushes his way in front of
him.

CUT TO:

A profile shot of Stevie and Mel. Above
the blistering drum'n'bass track we can
just hear...

    STEVIE
  (talking into Mel's ear)
  Calm down, Mel...I'll deal with it!

    MEL
  (manic, shouting)
  Did you hear what he just did?
  (POINTS AT DJ) He fucking name-
  checked that poxy station!

Mel tries to push past Stevie, who blocks
him. People nearby look over,
automatically moving back and giving
trouble a bit of space to happen in.
Coming through the crowd towards Mel and
Stevie we see Kev, one of the new
security team.

    STEVIE
  (firm)
  I said *I'll* deal with it...you
  handle security, and *my*
  responsibility's the talent, OK?

Stevie pats Mel on the shoulders, pastes
on a theatrical smile and leans forward.

>STEVIE
>And you don't *ever* fuck with the
>talent, Mel...they're what brings
>the punters in, right?

>KEV (O.S.)
>Everything alright, Mel?

CAMERA PULLS BACK TO INCLUDE KEV.

>MEL
>No problems, Kev...this is Stevie,
>he looks after the — what did you
>call them?

>STEVIE
>The talent, Mel, (TURNS TO WALK OFF)
>not something you'd know a lot
>about.

Mel's right eye twitches slightly as
Stevie walks away. He turns to Kev, who's
got that security man 'I see nothing and
everything' face on.

>MEL
>Good work...you did good.

CUT TO:

51 INT. TRANSIT VAN — FRONT — NIGHT   51

Martin, Phil and Billy are coming towards
the end of their shift. It's late,
they've spent another Friday night in the
back of a cramped Transit and it's about
time to call it a day.

CAMERA ON THE FRONT OF THE VAN:

        BILLY
    (turning in the driver's seat)
    We never had a look for that new
    station, did we? That wossname...
    Reel FM. It's only 2 o'clock, not
    too late to see if they got on air.

        MARTIN (O.S.)
    (from the back)
    What was their frequency?

        BILLY
    103.5, boss.

CUT TO:

In the back of the van, Martin is
watching as Phil tunes the equipment to
Reel FM's wavelength. As he does so a
blast of music comes out of the speakers.

> PHIL
> Up and running. Want me to
> take bearings?

> MARTIN
> Can't be arsed...we'll have another
> go tomorrow night.

> PHIL
> I bloody hate these double shifts.

> MARTIN
> Think of the overtime.

> BILLY (O.S.)
> Can we knock off now?

> MARTIN
> (stretches and yawns)
> Home, James — and don't spare the
> horses.

CUT TO:

The clock on the wall says 3.30, the
looks on the faces of the people — Sy,
Tom, Jo, CC and Stella — flopped about
the room say 'knackered'. Tom and Stella
are asleep, and it's quiet, except for a
low grade white noise in the background.

     CC
Turn the radio off, Jo...we're not
on the air any more.

Jo reaches out a bare foot and prods the
off button. The hissing stops. Down the
corridor we see the door to the studio
open and Nick come out with two guys we
haven't seen before. As they reach the
front door...

     SY
(waves)
Thanks, guys, see you tomorrow.

     JO
Tomorrow...Jesus, I've got to get
home. (SITS UP) Jase, have you
called that taxi or what?

     JASON
It'll be here in a minute,

babe...we're squeezing Tom in,
aren't we?

Somewhere in the room a mobile phone
starts playing a bizarre version of the
1812 Overture.

    JASON
That'll be the cab...wake the
sleeping beauties and let's go —
Sy, it's been real. (GRINS AND GIVES
HIM A BEAR HUG) Later.

    SY
Now we know what FM stands for.

    NICK
What's that?

    SY
Fucking marvellous!

CUT TO:

54 INT. MINICAB — NIGHT   54

Nick and Stella have been dropped off,
and so has Tom. Jason and Jo are sitting
together, but not close. He has his arm
lightly round her shoulder, but there's

quite obviously a tension between them.

> JASON
>
> Is it something I've done?

> JO
>
> Is what something you've done?

> JASON
>
> You don't seem very happy.

> JO
>
> And that has to be about you, does it?

> JASON
>
> I just thought—

> JO
>
> Think about this — there's more to
> *my* life than just you and me, not
> everything revolves around *us*.

> JASON
> (reasonable)
>
> Why are you so angry...so tense all
> the time lately? We haven't really
> *talked* for ages, we've just argued
> ...it's like...

JO
(interrupts)
...It's like being bloody married,
that's what you make it sound
like.

Jo leans forward to speak to the
Pakistani driver.

JO
Could you stop at the next corner,
please? Thanks. (TURNS BACK TO
JASON)

JASON
(holding in)
I was *actually* going to say that
you seem to spend more time talking
to Sy than me.

JO
Oh grow up, Jason!

The minicab pulls up by the kerb and Jo
opens the door.

JO
We'll split this, OK? Here's a
fiver, give me the change tomorrow.

Jo gets out of the car and closes the door. Jason slides over and rolls down the window.

> JASON
> Don't just walk out, Jo...come back to mine, let's talk...please?

> JO
> I'm tired, Jason...I need to go to bed. I'll see you tomorrow.

Jo turns away and starts to walk off. Jason almost calls after her, but turns and sits back. The minicab moves off. Jo stops walking and watches it drive off. Jason doesn't turn round to look after her.

Jo digs her hand into her bag for a couple of seconds, trying to find something in the jumble. Eventually, her hand comes out holding her phone. Standing in the street she looks at it, then puts it back in her bag and starts walking.

A few moments later she stops and takes it out again, chewing her lip. Finally, she dials a number and waits as it rings.

> JO
> (impatient)
> Come on...Sy, sorry, did I wake

144

you? (PAUSE) I'm just walking up to
my house...No, he went home...Look,
oh god, I don't know why I'm doing
this, it's...

Jo sits down on a low garden wall, wiping
away a tear.

    JO
No, I'm OK, I just need to
talk...(PAUSE)...no, not *now*!
When's everyone coming round
tomorrow? Oh, right, CC's stayed
...yeah, I know the café, the one
by the bus stop? See you there
around midday?

Jo ends the call, puts the phone back in
her bag and stays sitting on the wall,
leaning forward, elbows on her knees and
her head in her hands.

CUT TO:

55 INT. GREASY SPOON CAFÉ — DAY   55

Sy and Jo are sitting opposite each other
at a table near the front of a pretty
scuzzy caff. Sy is wearing dark glasses
and has a cup of black coffee in front of
him; Jo, smoking a cigarette, looks like

she hasn't slept and has an ashtray in
front of her.

POV LOOKING OVER SY'S SHOULDER AT JO, TOWARDS THE
BACK OF THE CAFÉ.

     SY
  You smoke too much...have I told
  you that?

     JO
  You, and the rest. Look, I'm sorry
  I dragged you out, but I've been
  thinking a lot about what you
  said...about me and Jason, about
  only being together so's I could be
  near Nick.

     SY
  Yeah?

     JO
  Yeah, and you're right...and
  knowing you're right makes it
  really hard at the moment.

     SY
  How so?

POV CHANGES SO WE'RE NOW LOOKING OVER JO'S SHOULDER
AT SY. BEHIND HIM WE CAN SEE THE STREET.

                JO
     We're all together so much...it's,
     like, *major* pressure. And I can
     feel Stella looking daggers all the
     time.

                SY
     What can I do?

                JO
     You can't do anything, Sy...except
     tell me that I'm not overreacting,
     that I'm doing the right thing.

POV SWITCHES BACK TO LOOKING OVER SY'S SHOULDER
AT JO.

                SY
     (worried)
     What're you planning, for
     chrissake?

                JO
     Don't worry, nothing serious...I've
     just decided to go back to college.
     Well, actually, to go to college
     ...I kind of let that slip along
     the way, but I've got all the As I
     need, my portfolio's not *bad*.

                    147

POV SWITCHES BACK TO LOOKING OVER JO'S SHOULDER
AT SY.

            SY
    Where would you go?

            JO
    (sits back)
    Glasgow?

            SY
    (sits forward)
    Know what? I think it sounds like a
    smooth idea. Clean slate, moving
    on, all that stuff.

BEHIND SY WE SEE A SINGLE-DECKER BUS, SLOWING DOWN
ALMOST TO A HALT IN THE SATURDAY MORNING TRAFFIC AS
IT GOES PAST THE CAFÉ. JASON IS SITTING IN A WINDOW
SEAT...

CUT TO:

56 INT. BUS — DAY   56

    We're looking at Jason's profile. Through
    the window we can see the café, and the
    table at which Sy and Jo are sitting. Sy
    has his back to us, but we can clearly
    see Jo — she's reaching out and squeezing

Sy's hand. At which point, Jason looks round.

CUT TO:

57 EXT. BUS — DAY   57

Shot from outside the bus, we see Jason's face. It turns from recognition, to puzzlement, to disbelief — and then the traffic speeds up and the bus disappears out of shot.

CUT TO:

58 INT. GREASY SPOON CAFÉ — DAY   58

Side shot of Sy and Jo at the table. Sy's finishing his coffee and Jo's putting her cigarettes and lighter in her bag.

    JO
Thanks, Sy...you're a real friend, you know that?

    SY
(pushing back his chair and getting up)
No problem...always fancied myself as an Agony Uncle!

CUT TO:

59 INT. GRAN'S BLOCK — OUTSIDE LIFTS — DAY   59

Jo and Sy are waiting for one of the
lifts to reach the ground floor, pressing
buttons and scanning the indicator lights,
either of which may or may not work.
    Then one set of lift doors opens and as
they move towards it CC steps out.

        CC
Hi, Jo (GIVES HER A HUG)...where'd
you disappear to, Sy?

        SY
(glances at Jo)
Had to get to the building society
before it closed...met Jo on the
way back and had a cup of coffee at
that rough place on the High
Street.

        CC
(smiles as he exits)
Hope you took antibiotics...(TURNS)
oh, nearly forgot, left your keys
upstairs.

        SY
Didn't you lock up?

Jo sees the lift doors closing and runs
to stop them, but she's too late.

> CC
> Jason's up there...don't know
> what's the matter with him though,
> he's rancid this morning.

CC waves and leaves. Sy and Jo go back to
punching buttons and waiting for a lift.

> SY
> Did you say something to him last night?

> JO
> No...well, yeah...I did say there
> was more to my life than him and
> me, and I kind of told him to grow
> up.

> SY
> He'll be a happy bunny, then.

CUT TO:

60 INT. VENUE — DAY   60

We're in Concrete. Chaz and Mel are
running a debriefing session with the
security teams on how the previous night
went.

CHAZ

...good night last night, no
trouble anywhere — that right, Mel?

Mel nods.

CHAZ

Before I forget, Mel has asked me
to remind you that the DJs and MCs
have been asked, very nicely, not
to mention any radio stations we
don't have a deal with...you'll get
a list later and just come and tell
either of us if you hear anything
you shouldn't.

And finally, even though there was
no sign of anyone remotely
connected to Big Elliot, let's not
get lazy.

Tonight's our big night and there's
going to be more of everything in
here — booze, birds and trouble
...so keep it extra-sharp.

Communication test at 5. Until
then, relax...

As Chaz and Mel watch the security guys
filter away, Chaz turns.

CHAZ

And you...you keep your stupid

temper on a leash...don't lose it
in front of the punters.

    MEL
(interrupts)
Did that smug little snot rag rat
on me?

    CHAZ
If you mean Stevie, no he didn't.

    MEL
(frowns)
So how...

    CHAZ
I was looking at last night's CCTV
footage, wasn't I, checking to see
if all the cameras are working, and
I happened to see it. OK?

    MEL
I was just—

Mel sees the look on Chaz's face and
realises that it's agreement the man
wants to hear, not excuses.

     MEL
(slightly shifty)
I'm cool, Chaz...eyes on the ball,
24/7.

     CHAZ
Better make sure they are, 'cos Mr
Sanders is chewing the wallpaper at
the *thought* of Big E doing
anything, so God knows what he'll
be like if he actually tries.

CUT TO:

61 INT. OFFICE — EVENING   61

At the Radiocommunications Agency
offices, Martin's walking towards us down
a corridor in the process of putting on
his jacket. As he passes an open door a
voice calls out to him.

     MR SIMMONS (O.S.)
Martin?

Martin stops, backtracks and looks
through the doorway.

     MARTIN
Eddy?

POV CHANGES TO INSIDE MR SIMMONS'S OFFICE.

MR SIMMONS
(sits back)
Haven't had a catch-up lately...you
got a moment?

MARTIN
(looks at his watch)
Just on my way out, Eddy...the boys
are waiting downstairs with the
van.

MR SIMMONS
OK, we'll talk later...by the way,
did you hear about that bloke who
was running Street FM, what was his
name?

MARTIN
Noddy Bevan.

MR SIMMONS
(nods)
Yeah, him...well he's suing us!

MARTIN
Get away! What the hell for?

MR SIMMONS
Cruelty to animals, would you
believe...he's chancing his arm
with one of those 'no win, no pay'

outfits — he's not back on the air
again, is he?

> MARTIN
> Not as far as we know...could have
> changed the station's name. We've
> picked up a couple of new ones in
> the last few days...In fact, we've
> got one on the top of our list
> tonight.

> MR SIMMONS
> (moves uncomfortably in
> his chair)
> Be careful...

CUT TO:

62 EXT. CAR PARK — EVENING   62

Martin exits the building. Phil and Billy
are waiting, joining him as he walks to
the parked Transit.

> BILLY
> (dropping cigarette and
> stepping on it)
> What kept you?

> MARTIN
> A quick chat with Mr Simmons. (OPENS

SIDE SLIDE DOOR) You'll never guess
what.

      PHIL
What?

      MARTIN
Noddy's only suing us for cruelty
to his bloody dogs.

Phil and Billy crack up at the thought —
Phil joining Martin in the back, Billy
opening the driver's door.

CAMERA FOLLOWS PHIL AND MARTIN.

      MARTIN
D'you think Noddy could be behind
that Reel FM outfit?

      PHIL
Why would he change the name?

      BILLY (O.S.)
Why does a dog lick its balls?

      MARTIN
Because it can.

POV OUTSIDE THE VAN. AS IT DRIVES AWAY WE CAN HEAR
LAUGHTER.

CUT TO:

63 INT. GRAN'S FLAT — THE STUDIO   63

Jason and Nick are in the studio, going
through the running order for the night's
broadcast.

> JASON
> After you, we've got Sy, Aisha,
> Mickey, Donna and Trev...Davey's
> let me down on the decks, says he's
> got to go to his sister's
> engagement party, so I'm going to
> have to do two sets.

> NICK
> That why you're so pissed off?

Jason sits back in his chair and takes
off his 'phones.

> JASON
> Gimme a fag.

> NICK
> You gave up.

Jason makes a rapid beckoning movement
and Nick throws his pack of cigarettes to
him.

JASON
I think Jo and Sy've got a thing
going on.

NICK
What?

Jason takes a cigarette out of the pack,
but doesn't light it.

JASON
She's been really bitchy to me
recently...haven't you noticed? She
made that big thing, the other day,
of not coming to the pub with us
and getting a lift with Sy. And
then I saw them together in that
caff on the High Street this
morning.

NICK
(registers disbelief)
You sure?

JASON
What...that I saw them? Positive,
can't miss that hair.

NICK
Jo and Sy? No, doesn't fit. Sy
wouldn't do that, must be something

else...(PAUSE)...Why's she been
giving you a hard time?

JASON
You tell me...

NICK
Know what you mean...Stella's been
acting weird lately, too.

Nick reaches over and takes the fag out
of Jason's hand and lights it. Jason
smiles wryly and chucks the pack back.

NICK
These women...why do they always
have to complicate things up?
Why can't they just...I dunno, just
not always look for bloody *reasons*
for everything...Stel's got it into
her head I'm still sweet on Jo.
Figure *that* one out.

JASON
You're not, are you?

NICK
(frowns)
Jason! Are you going paranoid, or
what?

JASON

Just because you're paranoid
doesn't mean someone *isn't*
following you. (PUTS ON 'PHONES)
Let's get the show on the road,
shall we, 'cos this is the only
thing that's keeping my head
together right now...

CUT TO:

64 INT. VENUE — FOYER — NIGHT   64

Mel comes out of a door marked 'Private'
and into the main foyer. He stands at the
edge of the crowd, surveying the scene
for a moment and then spots Kev scanning
the room as he talks into his mobile.
Mel's face registers displeasure and he
moves into the crush.

MEL
(coming up behind Kev)
No fucking personal calls on duty,
sunshine!

Kev spins round, taken by surprise.

KEV
Mel, sorry! Ah, I forgot to turn it
off...it was my mum.

161

As Kev makes to turn the phone off, Mel
grabs it.

> MEL
> (sneers)
> Piss off, *Mum*!

Mel jabs the off button and hands the
phone back to Kev.

> MEL
> Tell your 'Mum' not to ring you at
> work, and remember the bleeding
> rules, OK?

CUT TO:

65 INT. PUB — NIGHT   65

Big Elliot's right-hand man, Frank, is
sitting near the back of a pub, looking
at his mobile as if it smells bad. Next
to him, Dennis is concentrating on
rolling a cigarette.

> FRANK
> That Mel bloke, he needs some
> serious sorting out...just grabbed
> Kev's phone and told someone he
> *thought* was Kev's mum to piss off!

DENNIS

So...(LICKS THE PAPER) no stress,
you ain't Kev's mum.

FRANK

Little pillock didn't *know* that,
did he?

DENNIS

True...(ROLLS UP) but I did tell
you this was a bad time to call the
man...him being at work an' all.

FRANK

I had to check everything was
kosher.

Dennis surveys his handiwork, nods at a
job well done and lights up.

DENNIS

And was it?

FRANK

He says so...that's not a spliff,
is it?

DENNIS

Not everyone from Jamaica a
Rastaman, Frank...

CUT TO:

Not exactly a party, but a very buzzy
gathering. A clock on the wall shows it's
2.30 a.m. and the night's going well.
Jason's on his second shift, but Tom,
Stella, Sy, Nick and Jo are there
relaxing, as are a couple of guest DJs
and MCs...

CAMERA PANS ROUND THE ROOM, FOLLOWING PIECES OF
BROKEN, INCONSEQUENTIAL CONVERSATION, STOPPING AS
ONE OF THE GUESTS ASKS IF THERE ARE ANY MORE CRISPS
OR NUTS.

CUT TO:

        JO
   Think we've run out...that was the
   end of the last packet I brought
   out whenever I brought it out.

        SY
   (faking major distress)
   Don't tell me! No munchies...oh no!

        JO
   Cut it out, Sy...I'll go and get
   some more — that place round the
   corner's still open, isn't it?

            SY
      (gets up)
      I'll come with you.

            NICK
      You're on in a couple of minutes,
      mate...you'd better let...

Nick catches Stella, mid pouring herself
another vodka and orange, drilling him
with her eyes.

            NICK
      ...um, you better let Tom go with
      you.

Nick shoots a look back at Stella. Sy
checks his watch.

            SY
      Don't time fly...OK, but while
      you're down there, (DIGS KEYS OUT
      OF HIS POCKET) could you get a tape
      out of the player in my car?
      Something I want Greg to hear.
      (THROWS KEYS TO JO) Thanks.

As Jo and Tom get up to go, the door to
the flat opens and CC comes in, grinning.
He has his backpack and helmet with him.

NICK

Where've you been all this time?

CC

Little errand.

SY

Oh yeah, we know you and your
'little errands', what you been up
to now?

CC

Just some flyering.

NICK

You been winding up the Violent
Brothers again?

JO

CC! Leave it out, guy. Look what
they did to Jason's dad's place!

CC

We don't *know* that was them.

JO

Bloody hell, CC, why d'you have to
treat *everything* like it's a
fucking game?

Without waiting for an answer, Jo exits, followed by Tom.

> CC
> (shrugs)
> Sor-eee...It was just a couple of hundred flyers in the bogs at Concrete...you know, for a laugh.

> NICK
> Man, if you'd got caught, they'd've trashed you.

> CC
> (cocky)
> But they didn't, did they?

CUT TO:

67 INT. ALL-NITE SHOPPERS' PARADISE — NIGHT   67

Tom and Jo are choosing packets of crisps and other snacks in the 24-hour Indian mini-market. The place is lit in the standard harsh, over-bright fluorescent strips, and bangra music is playing in the background.
The door bell ding-dongs and we see Billy walk in and go up to the counter.

Jo and Tom don't really take much notice
of the newcomer, but go and queue up
behind him.

POV OVER BILLY'S SHOULDER.

> BILLY
> Packet of Bensons, these chocolates
> (PICKS UP THREE DIFFERENT BARS) and
> d'you do coffee? Like to take away?

> KUMAR
> (nods towards a filter machine)
> Might be a bit stewed, mate.

> BILLY
> Gimme three milky ones, will you?
> Two sugars each. Just need the buzz,
> mate, we've still got a couple of
> hours before we knock off — can't
> do our job if you're falling
> asleep.

> KUMAR
> (making coffees)
> What you do?

POV OVER KUMAR'S SHOULDER.

> BILLY
> (grins)
> We're the sheriff's posse, mate.
> (MAKES A PRETEND GUN WITH HIS FINGERS) We
> catch the bad guys, you know, the
> pirates.

Behind the counter, Kumar darts a glance
at his cassette player, which Billy
notices. Behind Billy, Jo and Tom freeze.

> BILLY
> Not pirate tapes, mate — pirate
> *radio*.

Kumar looks relieved as he puts the three
cups in front of Billy, hands him a blue
plastic bag and then tills up.

> BILLY
> You can do what you like with
> tapes, that's not our department —
> what's the damage?

POV OVER BILLY'S SHOULDER.

> KUMAR
> £7.80, mate.

> BILLY
> Bloody hell...(HANDS OVER A £10 NOTE)

```
    ...I'll have to give up
    drinking coffee, eh!

POV OVER KUMAR'S SHOULDER.

We see Billy take his stuff and go,
leaving us looking at Jo and Tom. Jo,
looking nervous, puts the basket she's
carrying up on the counter.

        JO
    (indicating the door with
    her head)
    Why don't you, like, wait for me
    outside?

        TOM
    What f— Oh, right, outside...see
    you there.

Kumar's not paying them any attention, a
song he likes is playing and he's
counting out the contents of Jo's basket.

        KUMAR
    That'll be £4.55.

Jo hands over a fiver, takes the bag and
the change Kumar gives her and exits.
```

CUT TO:

68 EXT. STREET — NIGHT   68

Jo comes out of the shop, looking left
and right, trying to locate Tom.

>   TOM (O.S.)
>   Jo!

Jo turns, sees Tom beckoning to her and
runs up to him.

>   JO
>   Where'd he go?

>   TOM
>   (nods)
>   That white Transit over there...I
>   saw inside when he gave them their
>   coffees...it's stuffed full of
>   equipment.

>   JO
>   Better not stand round looking at
>   them.

>   TOM
>   What're we gonna do?

Jo, digging round in her bag, gets her
phone out. Looking at it frowning, she
presses the on button.

    JO
  Shit!

    TOM
What's the matter?

    JO
I'm so brain dead sometimes...flat
bloody battery again...got yours?

    TOM
Didn't bring it.

    JO
OK...OK...

Jo snaps her fingers, thinking, then...

    JO
Here's what we'll do. (GIVES TOM
THE BAG) Go back and tell them
what's happened, tell them to come
off the air *right now*!

Jo then turns and starts to run off.

172

TOM
Where are you going?

JO
(hisses)
To get the transmitter!

Jo waves and disappears round a corner.

TOM
You can't!

He hesitates, looks at the white van,
looks after Jo, torn about what to do.
Major dilemma — whatever decision he
makes has its downside. In the end he
goes the opposite way to Jo.

69 EXT./INT. STREET/BLOCK — NIGHT   69

Series of JUMP CUTS, following Tom as he:
— runs hell for leather to the tower
  block;
— arrives in the foyer and punches
  buttons, but can't wait for the lifts
  so goes for the stairs;
— skirts past a couple snogging,
  apologising as he goes;
— arrives at the flat door, exhausted,
  and presses the bell.

CUT TO:

70 INT. GRAN'S FLAT — MAIN ROOM — NIGHT   70

Nick opens the door and Tom staggers in.

    NICK
What's the matter, Tom? (LOOKS OUT
THE DOOR)...Where's Jo?

    TOM
(getting his breath back)
She's...she's gone to get the
transmitter.

Everyone in the room has now gathered
round in a loose circle, with Nick and
Tom at its centre.

    SY
(confused)
She *what*? Why'd she do that?

    TOM
(still breathless)
DTI...saw them down there in the
street — she said to get off...get
off the bloody air!

    NICK
Jesus! She's gone up there on her

own? How the *hell's* she gonna get
on to the roof?

CAMERA ON:

SY
She's got my keys.

A moment's pause as this information
sinks in, then...

NICK
I gotta go...where are those
torches?

STELLA
(shocked)
Nick, what're you doing?

Sy gets a torch out of one of the black
bags and gives it to Nick. We can see
that Stella's a little unsteady on her
feet...

STELLA
Nick? Listen to me...don't go!

NICK
Leave it out, Stel...she could be in
real trouble up there. Sy, go and
tell Jase to shut the house down.

175

And Tom, unhook the microwave stuff
...just in case they come up here.

As Nick turns to go for the door, Stella
lunges at him, holding him. She's crying
now.

>   NICK
> Stel, Stel, come on, this is
> silly...let go, OK?...It's bad up
> there, I've got to get after her.

>   STELLA
> (pushes back, angry)
> Why *you*? Why not someone else? It's
> always been you and her, hasn't it,
> you bastard!

>   NICK
> You're drunk, Stel.

Like a snake, Stella's arm whips out and
slaps Nick in the face. In the shocked
silence, Nick twists the Yale lock open
and exits, slamming the door behind him.
Sy nods to CC that he should do
something with Stella, who's now sobbing
silently, hugging herself. As Sy runs off
down the corridor, Tom goes over to the
balcony.

CUT TO:

71 INT. GRAN'S FLAT — THE STUDIO — NIGHT   71

Jason and Greg, one of the guest MCs,
are doing their stuff as the door is
flung open and Sy hurtles in.

    SY
Get off the air, Jase!

Jason and Greg look round, caught
unawares by the sudden intrusion.

    JASON
(putting a hand over the mic)
We're *on* the bloody air, Sy...what
the hell's going on?

    SY
The DTI's downstairs, trawling...
Jo's gone up the other block to get
the transmitter...Nick's gone after
her...

    GREG
(not covering his mic)
Hit the switches, bro!

CUT TO:

Phil's hunched over, pressing his 'phones
tighter to his head, Martin has picked up
a set and has one half pressed to his
ear.

      MARTIN
What're they saying?

      PHIL
We've been sussed, somehow...
(PAUSE) They're going off the
air, any moment. (PAUSE) Did you
get that, Martin?

      MARTIN
Yeah, but there are *six* blocks on
the estate, they could be going up
any one of them...how the hell are
we going to watch 'em all?

      BILLY (O.S.)
Boss? Remember that chancer we
picked up at the Street FM raid?
The lad you had to let go?

      MARTIN
Yeah? Why?

POV CHANGES, WE'RE LOOKING OUT OF THE FRONT OF THE VAN.

> BILLY
> He's just come tearing out of
> Meadowbank like his arse was on
> fire.

> MARTIN
> Can you keep him in sight? I'm
> gonna give the local boys a call
> and see if they've got anything in
> the air.

CUT TO:

73 INT. BLOCK — LIFT — NIGHT 73

Jo's in one of the lifts; she's standing
in one of the corners near the controls
and she looks like she's having second
thoughts about what she's doing.
The lift halts and the doors open. A
man — mid to late 30s, nerdy, Trekkie
type — pokes his torso in, holding the
doors apart.

> MAN
> You, um, going up or down?

        JO
   (nervous)
   Down — I mean up...up. Up to the top.

The man walks into the lift.

        MAN
   I'm going down, but at least this
   one's going somewhere...

Jo presses the close-door button and the
lift starts going again. She smiles at
the man and looks away. He clears his
throat.

        MAN
   QasStaH nuq?

        JO
   (confused)
   Sorry?

        MAN
   I said 'what's happening?' in
   Klingon...I'm learning it, you
   know, on the Net?

        JO
   That's nice.

          MAN
     It's the fastest growing language
     in the universe, they say...it was
     invented for *Star Trek*, the TV
     series.

          JO
     Really?

          MAN
     HiSlaH! That was 'yes'.

FADE TO:

74   INT. LIFT — DOORS OPENING — NIGHT   74

As the doors open on to the corridor we
see Jo coming through the gap like a
draught.

          MAN
     ...*lojmIt yipoSmoH!* See, I just
     said 'open the door!' and it
     did...Bye then.

          JO
     (waves)
     Bye.

Jo watches the lift doors close, then
digs in her handbag.

                    181

                    JO
          (shaking her head)
          'Klingon'? (FINDS KEYS) Jesus!

The camera now follows Jo as she looks
for the door to the emergency stairs and
goes in.

CUT TO:

75 INT. VENUE — NIGHT   75

We're in the main office at Concrete.
It's a fairly large room dominated by a
wall of CCTV monitors in front of which
sit two men in shirt-sleeves. The other
dominant feature is a large beige-
coloured safe in a corner, its door is
slightly open. The place is furnished in
reasonably new, mid-range office
furniture.
     Mel is there, along with a couple of
the security guys, and it's obvious that
Mel is stressed about something.

                    MEL
          (waving flyers)
          Where'd you find these?

                DON
    There was some in all the toilets,
    men's and women's, and Terry (NODS
    AT THE OTHER MAN) found a load
    stuffed in the rack in the foyer.

                MEL
    In the fucking *foyer*? (SWINGS
    ROUND) Did you lot not see
    anything?

The two men in shirt-sleeves turn to look
at Mel.

            1ST CCTV MAN (TONY)
    (calm)
    They were found *in* the cubicles,
    Mel...we don't film people on the
    shitter, it's against the law —
    invasion of privacy.

                MEL
    (sarcastic)
    What about the foyer then, we can
    film *there*, can't we?

Behind the two men, who are still looking
at Mel, we can see one of the screens
flicker and go blank. It was showing the
outside of the building.

          MEL
(addressing Don)
Can you believe the nerve of these
little shits?

          TONY
(jerks thumb behind him at
a screen)
As it happens, the camera angle we
have down there, see? People
standing at the rack have their
backs to us...could be doing
anything.

Everyone looks at the foyer monitor. The
other CCTV man spots the blank screen and
starts trying to get it back via his
keyboard.

          2ND CCTV MAN (COL)
Tony? One of the monitors seems to
have gone on the fritz...

          TONY
Which one, Col?

          COL
Rear entrance...

          MEL
Some little scumbag trying to let

his mates in for free — Don? You
two get down there and sort it,
now.

Don and the other security man leave the
office.

    TONY
Why're you getting so wound up
about a few flyers, Mel? Hardly
seems worth it.

    MEL
(his back to the door)
It's worth it because we have
deals, Tony...only certain parties
are allowed in here, and these lot
(TEARS UP A REEL FM FLYER) aren't
bloody one of them!

In the background, we can hear the tell-
tale beeping as someone enters the four-
digit code to open the office door.

    MEL
We let any old riff-raff in, we got
no control, right?

Behind him, the office door opens and
three ski-masked men silently slip into
the room. Two are carrying a sawn-off

shotgun, one covering Tony and Col, the other looking after Mel. The third, a younger man, has a backpack on, which he quickly takes off and unzips. Mel, dropping the flyers he'd been holding, looks like he's just entered an alternate universe.

FRANK
How right you are, Mel my old son
...now, you can make this easy, or you can make it difficult — and you two over there with all the buttons, that means you don't touch *nothing*, understand?

It takes Mel a second or two to get over the shock of what he's seeing, but only a second or two.

MEL
You're Big E's crew, aren't you...I don't fucking believe it.

FRANK
Seeing's believing, sunshine, now be a good boy and go and sit down at that desk. Liam, do your stuff.

Mel looks at the twin black holes at the

end of the barrels Frank is pointing
right at him.

>   MEL
>   (as he moves backwards to
>   the chair)
>   You won't get away with this.

>   FRANK
>   Just watch me...Hurry it up, Liam!

Liam rips open a large roll of silver
gaffer tape he's taken out of his
backpack and wraps it very tight half a
dozen times round Mel and the chair. Mel,
looking disoriented as the process is
repeated on his legs, watches Frank walk
over to the safe.

>   FRANK
>   See that, Den? They knew we were
>   coming and left it open for us.
>   (LOOKS OVER HIS SHOULDER) Slap
>   some on his mouth, we won't be
>   needing the combination.

>   MEL
>   (revelation)
>   That's it...this is an inside job,
>   isn't it? You had the combination
>   for the bloody door!

FRANK
Shut him up, will you?

While Liam finishes off Mel by slapping
some tape over his mouth, then moves on
to Tony and Col, Frank takes the backpack
and begins filling it with what's in the
safe. We can see wads of money, some
powder and pill-filled plastic bags.
    Frank stands up, checks his watch, then
zips up the backpack.

FRANK
You finished, Liam? (LIAM NODS) Just
about 45 seconds, nice one. Let's
go...Cover the door, Den——

Frank helps Liam on with the backpack,
noticing the Reel FM flyers Mel had
dropped when they came in.

FRANK
(picking up a couple of flyers)
There you go, Liam, something to
listen to on the way home.

Dennis opens the door, checks and nods
for them to go through. As he's about to
exit, Dennis stops and points the shotgun
at Mel, whose eyes almost pop out of his
head as he frantically tries to twist

himself out of the way.

SLOW MOTION/CLOSE-UP OF DENNIS PULLING THE TRIGGER.

There's a loud double click.

> DENNIS
> Bang-bang!

He closes the door.

CUT TO:

76 INT. CORRIDOR — NIGHT   76

We see Liam and Frank, now with their ski
masks off, waiting for Dennis. He rips
his mask off as soon as he's out, putting
his shotgun away in a special underarm
holster. As he's doing that Liam cuts the
wires to the door's electronic lock.

> LIAM
> That should keep 'em in for a bit.

> FRANK
> Back door, fast — Kev should be at
> the car by now.

The three men move off down the corridor,
shooting glances over their shoulders.

FRANK
(smiling)
Bang-bang! You're a cruel bastard, Dennis.

CUT TO:

77 INT. — BLOCK — NIGHT   77

Nick comes tearing into the entrance of the other block, almost knocking over the man from the lift.

NICK
Sorry, mate — you OK?

Without waiting for an answer, Nick runs to the lifts.

MAN
(forcefully)
*Heghlu'meH QaQ jajvam!**

Nick manages to catch the lift the man's just got out of, and he runs in, punching the top button. We see the doors close.

CUT TO:

*Today is a good day to die!

78 INT. CORRIDOR — NIGHT   78

   The camera's in the same position,
   looking at the lift doors. The only
   reason we can tell we've moved is that
   the graffiti has changed.
      The doors open and we see Nick smashing
   the wall of the lift with the flat of his
   palm.

            NICK
      Bloody thing!

   With one last kick at the door, he exits
   the lift and runs for the emergency
   stairs.

   CUT TO:

79 INT. STAIRWELL — NIGHT   79

   Shot from the very top, looking down the
   stairwell. We can hear Nick running up
   towards us, occasionally see a hand grab
   the banisters.

   CUT TO:

80 EXT. ROOF — NIGHT   80

   We're on the roof, with the open doorway
   centre screen. We can hear footsteps

running, getting louder. We can also hear
— just — a WHUPP-WHUPP-WHUPP sound in the
background, growing steadily louder.

Nick appears, out of breath and
sweating. Stumbling on to the roof, he
looks around.

>   NICK
> Jo!

He immediately sees that the louvre is
open and he runs over to the vent tower,
the WHUPP-WHUPP-WHUPP sound getting louder
and louder.

>   NICK
> Are you there, Jo?

Nick's just about to start climbing the
rungs up to the open louvre when Jo's
head and shoulders appear, her blonde
hair almost bright against the blackness
behind her.

>   JO
> Come on up and give me a hand — I
> can't get the bloody thing off the
> wall!

Jo leans out, reaching down a hand...at
which point there's a blinding flash and

the two of them are inside a column of
hard, white light that almost seems to
freeze them in its beam.

>   LOUD HAILER (O.S.)
>   STAY WHERE YOU ARE...

CUT TO:

81 INT. GRAN'S FLAT — MAIN ROOM   81

CC, Greg, Sy and Jason are gathered round
Tom, who is looking through his
binoculars out of the French windows.
Stella is sitting on the sofa, nursing a
drink, smoking a cigarette and apparently
ignoring the excitement. In the
background is the same insistent WHUPP-
WHUPP-WHUPP sound.

>   CC
>   What's going on up there, Tom?

>   TOM
>   Like I can see!   .

>   SY
>   (looking up in the sky)
>   Bloody hell!

>   CC
>   What?

SY
(points)
Helicopter.

TOM
I *think* I can see Nick...he's by
the vent tower.

One moment the sky is that inky blue-
black of a big city night, the next it's
like someone has ripped it with a knife
and let the daylight in.

TOM
Jeez...that's amazing...they're
like bloody Romeo and Juliet!

CC
Let me see, bro. (TOM HANDS OVER
THE BINOCULARS) Incredible! Jase,
quick, you've gotta have a look!

Everyone's so intent on witnessing the
events unfolding on the roof that no one
notices Stella getting up and leaving the
room.

JASON
(with binoculars)
What did she think she was going to
do up there...rip the transmitter

194

off the wall with her bare hands?

        TOM
    (pointing at the ground)
    Look...there's a police car, and
    the van we saw...(TURNS) Stella,
    come and...Stella? Anybody see
    where she went?

CAMERA QUICK CUTS FROM FACE TO FACE AS THEY REALISE
THERE MAY BE A PROBLEM.

        SY
    She was pretty trolleyed, maybe...

Sy runs to the bedroom as Jason checks
the kitchen. Sy comes out shaking his
head.

        SY
    Not there.

Jason comes out of the kitchen.

        JASON
    The cutlery drawer was open.

        SY
    Shit! (LOOKS DOWN THE CORRIDOR)
    The bathroom!

At the end of the darkened corridor we
can see light coming out under the
bathroom door. Sy runs down to it, Jason
and the others close behind. He tries the
door. Locked.

> SY
> Stella? You in there? Come on,
> girl, open up now.

> STELLA (O.S.)
> (muffled)
> Go away...leave me alone.

> JASON
> Kick it down, Sy! Ferchrissake!

> SY
> Someone get me a screwdriver —
> quick!

Tom runs back up to the main room. Sy
turns back to the door.

> SY
> Stella, listen to me...don't do
> anything stupid in there...stuff
> was said, it can always be talked
> over — sticks and stones, girl,
> sticks and stones.

Tom comes back and slaps a screwdriver into Sy's waiting hand. He quickly inserts it into a small recess below the handle, turns it clockwise, then drops it on the floor. Taking a deep breath, Sy grabs the handle and pushes open the door.

POV CHANGES TO INSIDE THE BATHROOM.

Sy steps in, checks left — the bath's empty — looks right. Stella is sitting on the toilet, with the lid down. She's leaning forward, sobbing, a series of ragged slash marks visible on her left wrist, blood dripping on to the bathroom lino. In her right hand she's holding an old kitchen knife, which she lets drop as Jason looks round the door.

> SY
> Call an ambulance.

Stella slowly sits up, turning her pale, tear-stained face towards Sy and Jason.

> STELLA
> (exhausted)
> Oh God...I can't do *anything* right.

CUT TO:

82 EXT. VAN — REAR — NIGHT 82

The Transit is parked outside the
Bowman's Field block. Billy is leaning up
against the side and the sliding door is
open. Inside, we can see Martin talking
to someone on his mobile.

CAMERA ZOOMS IN ON MARTIN.

          MARTIN
    The Duty Officer rang you? Why?
    (PAUSE) Think he must be a bit of a
    panic-merchant, Eddy. No, it's all
    fine here. No, we didn't get the
    studio, they closed down too
    quick. Yeah, the local boys are up
    there now bringing them down.
    Phil went with them to check if the
    transmitter's there...(PAUSE)...
    Dunno what we can get 'em for,
    Eddy. Trespass? Criminal damage?
    Something like that I suppose.

o.s. we can hear another mobile going and
Billy comes into view, still holding the
phone to his ear.

BILLY
Gimme the drill case, boss...Phil's
found the box.

Billy takes the plastic case Martin hands
him and walks off towards the entrance.
The CAMERA stays on him, holding as he
goes in. Seconds later, the doors open
and two policemen come out with Jo and
Nick; the CAMERA follows them as they're
taken over to the police car and put in
the back.
The CAMERA pans back to Martin, still on
the phone. In the distance we can hear a
siren wailing.

MARTIN
...Yeah, another one bites the
dust...See you Monday, Eddy.

CUT TO:

83 EXT. GRAN'S FLAT — BALCONY — NIGHT   83

Jason is standing on the balcony, leaning
forward and looking over the edge.

JASON'S POV, LOOKING DOWN AT THE VAN AND POLICE
CAR.

We see the tiny figures of Jo and Nick

being put into the back of the police car, and then it drives away.

As Jason stands back up, we hear the bell go and Sy opening the door.

> AMBULANCE MAN (O.S.)
> Where is she?

> SY (O.S.)
> Back here.

Jason massages his eyes with both hands. He looks exhausted. Turning to look at the other block one last time, he sighs heavily and goes back into the flat.

CUT TO:

84 EXT. STREET — DAY   84

Sy is sitting on a graffiti-covered bench. It's not particularly sunny, but he has his sun glasses on, and he's sipping a cup of takeaway coffee from Coffee Republic, or some such. By his side is a plastic bag and another cup of coffee, with its lid on.

CAMERA STRAIGHT ON, SO SY AND THE BENCH TAKE UP THE FULL FRAME.

A figure walks in from the left of the
screen and sits down next to Sy. It's Nick.

>   SY
>   (handing Nick the coffee)
>   Yo, jailbird...what's freedom smell
>   like?

>   NICK
>   Beautiful, baby (TAKES CUP)
>   Thanks...sugar?

Sy hands Nick a couple of sachets and a
plastic stirrer.

>   NICK
>   (smiles tiredly)
>   If you were called Simone, I'd
>   seriously consider marrying you.

Nick carries on talking as he does the
coffee/sugar business.

>   NICK
>   So, what's up...you didn't say much
>   when they *finally* let me make a
>   call.

>   SY
>   Where to start...(LOOKS ROUND)
>   Where's Jo?

NICK
She rang her dad...he came and
picked her up. I bet she's in the
middle of one of those 'what's a
daughter of mine doing in a place
like that!' conversations...So,
fill me in.

Sy sits back and looks down to his left.
He picks up the plastic bag and gives it
to Nick.

SY
Your stuff, you know, phone and
things you left in the flat.

NICK
(takes the bag)
What aren't you telling me, Sy?

SY
(troubled)
No easy way to say this, Nick...
(PAUSE) Stella, uh, she cut her
wrist last night.

NICK
(concerned)
What on, man? How'd that happen?

          SY
    No, you don't get it...*she* did it.
    To herself.

The coffee cup stops midway to Nick's
mouth.

          NICK
    (confused)
    Suicide? She tried to commit
    suicide...no way...why?

          SY
    It was the Jo thing, man. You know
    she was all coming apart at the
    seams when you left, and it didn't help
    she kept on putting the vodka away.

CAMERA FOLLOWS AS SY GETS UP AND WALKS AS HE TALKS.

          SY
    Anyway, got a feeling the final
    straw was Tom looking through the
    binoculars when the spotlight hit
    you guys...he said it made you look
    like Romeo and Juliet. (SHRUGS) You
    did, man.
      She must've heard and flipped out,
    'cos the next thing we knew she'd
    locked herself in the bathroom with
    a knife.

NICK
Christ!

Nick puts down his coffee and lights a
cigarette.

NICK
(quietly)
Is she—

SY
The knife could hardly cut butter,
man...she made a nasty mess, but
the ambulance guy said we got to
her before she'd managed to get a
vein. (SHAKES HIS HEAD IN DISBELIEF)
She's at home now, far as I know.
  Jase went with her in the
ambulance, you'll have to get the
details from him.

NICK
Tried to call him before I called
you...just got his service.

A long pause, then, to no one in
particular...

NICK
What a fuck up...

Sy and Nick look at each other. Sy goes
back and sits next to him.

    SY
(hand on his shoulder)
It's no one's *fault*, bro...no way
to *ever* know everything going on
inside somebody's head.

    NICK
Jo and I had a long talk...she told
me everything.

    SY
(cautious)
Everything?

    NICK
About going back to college?

    SY
(slightly disappointed)
Oh, right.

    NICK
You know, trying to get a place at
Glasgow? She said she talked to you
about it.

                SY
She did...I said I thought it was a
good idea.

                NICK
Yeah, so do I...Been having similar
thoughts myself.

                SY
What?

                NICK
Man, *I'm* all out of cash — *we're*
all out of cash! That money I got
when my grandad died? My
investment? All gone...well, except
for beer money. There's certainly
not enough to get us a new rig.

Nick finishes his coffee and stubs his
cigarette in the cup.

                NICK
'Keep Britain tidy'...seemed like
such a great idea, didn't it?

                SY
What, Reel FM? It still *is* a great
idea!

NICK
True, but we were pretty crazed to
think we could do it without a
backer.

SY
(standing up)
Come on, I've got the car round the
corner, I'll drop you home.

NICK
I'd better go to Stella's first.
Did she say anything to you?

They both get up and walk off down the
street. As they go we hear:

SY
Apart from that she couldn't do
anything right? No, just cried.

NICK
Know what gets me?

SY
No, what?

NICK
I feel guilty, and I didn't even do
anything.

CUT TO:

85 INT. VENUE — OFFICE — DAY   85

The wall of CCTV monitors is on, with one
screen still blank. The safe door is
still open. Chaz is now sitting in the
chair behind the desk, a rolled up ball
of silver gaffer tape in front of him.
Standing by the door, which we can see
has had its lock broken, is Don the
security guy, and sitting opposite Chaz
is Mel. He looks nervous and has what
appears to be a square rash around his
mouth where the tape was ripped off.

        CHAZ
    Remember I told you Mr Sanders was
    chewing the wallpaper at the
    thought of Big E having a go? Well
    he's spitting brick dust now.
    And what he *really* wants — apart
    from a hundred K of his money and
    other merchandise back — is someone
    to blame.

        MEL
    We know who let them in — it was
    Kev...

CHAZ
(interrupts)
And who was in charge of security?
Who *hired* Kev? Which lazy, *feckless*
bastard didn't follow up a *single*
reference? And who left the bloody
safe door wide open?

Chaz turns to look at Don.

CHAZ
Any ideas, Don?

DON
Mr James, Mr Morton?

CHAZ
Correct. Mr Melvin James.

MEL
I was gonna...I just didn't have
time — you said—

CHAZ
Don't give me 'you said', you little
shit...you've got some *serious*
explaining to do.

MEL
Explaining?

Chaz picks up a remote, points it at a
TV/video combo set into the wall and
presses *play*.

The screen flicks on and we can see a
grainy black-and-white image of a room.
It's the office we're in and the video,
shot from high up in the ceiling, shows
Mel talking to Tony, tearing up a flyer.
Chaz turns the volume up.

> MEL
> (video)
> ...'This lot aren't bloody one of
> them! We let any old riff-raff in,
> we got no control, right?'

Behind him the door opens and two men
with sawn-offs come in, followed by a
third man.

> FRANK
> (video)
> 'How right you are, Mel my old son.'

Chaz turns off the vid and looks round at
Mel.

> CHAZ
> Mr Sanders was wondering how come
> they knew who you were? In fact,

he'll be here (LOOKS AT HIS WATCH)
any minute now to ask you himself.

Getting up, Chaz goes to the door.

    CHAZ
Make sure he doesn't go anywhere.

CUT TO:

86 INT. CHERRYTREE CAFÉ — DAY   86

Tom, CC, Jo, Jason and Sy are back in the
Cherrytree, the usual mess on the table.
Jo and Jason are sitting next to each
other, but not together. The bell on the
door rings as it opens.

    NICK
Sorry I'm late...I was looking for
the Reel Line phone, like you
asked, Sy...couldn't find it
anywhere at home.

Jimmy comes out of the kitchen carrying a
plate with an egg sandwich on it.

    JIMMY
Thought I'd got rid of all you
lot...How you been, Nick?

As he chats, Jimmy gives the sandwich to
Tom, picks up an empty plate from in
front of CC, empties an overflowing
ashtray on to it and gives the table a
cursory wipe with a dirty tea towel.

> NICK
> (still standing)
> Oh, you know, Jimmy, (GRINS WRYLY)
> up and down.

> JIMMY
> (exiting)
> *Etsi-jesti*...I know what you
> mean.

> SY
> (smiling after Jimmy)
> I think he's missed us...And don't
> worry about the phone, Stella
> called me earlier to say she found
> it with her stuff.

> JASON
> She was supposed to be taking the
> calls, you know, the other night.

> SY
> She said she'd be down sometime
> around now.

          NICK
     Yeah, we talked.

Jo slowly pushes her chair back and
stands, gathering up her bits and pieces.

          JO
     I've got to cut out, guys.

          JASON
     You don't have to go because——

          JO
     I'm not going *because* of anything,
     Jase...got to get ready for my
     evening class — my portfolio needs
     kickstarting if I'm ever going to
     get into Glasgow.

The CAMERA follows Jo as she walks behind
Jason — not touching him — squeezes Sy's
shoulder as she passes him and slaps
Nick's outstretched palm, then exits.
     A moment's silence, then...

          JASON
     We split...last night.

Jason takes one of CC's cigarettes out of
his pack and plays with it.

JASON
Unanimous decision.

Sympathetic nods and shrugs from the boys
as Nick sits down next to Jason and takes
the cigarette he's playing with. Too much
blood on the tracks for comfort here...
the subject, you feel, definitely needs
changing:

CC
Jo was saying, just before you got
here, all you two got was a
caution...how's that work out?

TOM
Yeah, remember when we looked it up on
the Net? It said you could get six
months inside and a £5,000 fine. How
d'you finesse that, Nick?

Nick picks up CC's lighter and flicks it
alight.

NICK
Up there on the roof? I thought
we'd had it, too...I mean,
helicopters, searchlights, cops,
the lot. It was like World War
bloody Three.

214

It wasn't until we got back to the
station that they let on they
really had nothing on us...the DTI
guy came by — it was the same bloke
who was there when they did Street
FM, the one who warned me off.

The others nod — they remember.

      NICK
He was quite straight, really...
said he knew we — Jo and me — were
to do with Reel FM, but that we'd
been lucky 'cos we went off the air
before they had time to trace the
transmission.
   Gave us a lecture about the
offences we'd been committing and
said the transmitter was being
confiscated.
   Turns out the cops couldn't even
get us on criminal damage 'cos (BOWS
IN SY'S DIRECTION) we had a key to
the lock and hadn't had to break
into the roof area or anything.

      TOM
What about the rig? Wasn't that a
bit of a giveaway? I mean, you were
up there trying to get it.

215

                    NICK
          They couldn't prove it was ours, or
          that we knew it was there, could
          they? We just denied any knowledge
          of it, said we were up there
          fooling around.

                    CC
          And that's it?

                    NICK
          (grins)
          Innocent until proven guilty, mate!

CC starts laughing and they all join in.

                    CC
          You jammy bastard!

CUT TO:

87 EXT. STREET — DAY   87

          We're pulled quite far back so that the
          front of a faintly run-down suburban
          North London house fills the screen.
          As the front door opens we ZOOM in on
          Stella as she exits, slamming the door
          behind her.
          She's dressed exactly as she was in
          intro SCENE 1.

                         216

CAMERA FOLLOWS BEHIND STELLA AS SHE WALKS AWAY DOWN
THE PAVEMENT.

We hear a mobile phone go off and see
Stella reach into her jacket pocket, get
it out and look at it before she answers.

> STELLA
> Yes, Mum? (PAUSE) Sorry, didn't
> mean to slam the door...or leave my
> light on...Yeah, 4.15 with Dr
> Taylor, Nick's going to come with
> me...(PAUSE)...there's nothing
> wrong with me, Mum...I was just
> drunk and a bit depressed, that's
> all...(SMILES) OK, *very* drunk and
> depressed, but I'm fine now, really...
> No, I don't know why we only talk
> like this on the phone, probably
> because we always shout at each
> other at home over something
> stupid...this way we just talk,
> don't we...Yeah, see you later,
> Mum. Love you.

As Stella puts the phone back in her
pocket there's another ring. She takes
her phone out, but it's obviously not the
one with the incoming call and she puts
it away again.

CAMERA PANS ROUND TO C/U OF STELLA'S FACE.

The phone keeps ringing. She stops
walking and opens her bag. Reaching in,
she brings out the Reel Line phone and
answers it.

> STELLA
> Hello?...Yeah, this is Reel FM...
> (PAUSE)...Stella, I'm Stella...Oh,
> hello, Frank...you have a call for
> me? Yeah, I'll hang on a moment.

Stella gets some chewing gum as she
waits, then the new caller obviously
comes on the line.

> STELLA
> Hi...yes, we just started last
> weekend, like it says on the flyers
> — what can I do? (PAUSE) Do I
> *own* it? No, it's a, you know,
> a...yeah, that's right, it's a
> cooperative. In fact, I'm on my way
> to meet the others now. (PAUSE)
> Are we looking for backing?

Stella takes the phone away from her ear
and looks at it, frowning in a perplexed,
slightly freaked-out way — like, 'How the
hell did he know?'

She puts the phone back to her ear...

>STELLA
>Could be. (PAUSE) Yeah, I'll,
>um, I'll talk to them and call you
>back — what's your name and number?
>Hang on.

CAMERA PULLS BACK.

Stella, phone tucked under her ear, gets
a biro and a piece of paper from her bag.

>STELLA
>Go on...Elliot...yeah, double L,
>one T, Williams...077, OK...yes,
>496...got it, we'll call you back
>Mr Williams...thanks.

Stella ends the call and stands still,
holding the phone by her side, for a
couple of beats.

CAMERA ZOOMS IN FOR A C/U ON HER FACE.

Stella shakes her head and smiles.

>STELLA
>Un-bloody-real.

>FADE OUT

Radio Radio: Cast

Reel FM team
Nick Foster/MC D-Cee
Stella Whitely
Jason Towne
Tom Cross
CC Oweyo
Jo Knight
Sy Redstone/Mr Standard MC
Stella's mother
Sheila Whitely
Guest MC on Reel FM
Greg Masters
Street FM
Noddy Bevan
Department of Trade and Industry (DTI)
Billy Mitchell
Martin Townsend
Phil Ripley
Mr Eddy Simmons
Violet Productions
Stevie Edwards
Mel James
Tyrone McRae
Chaz Morton
Sanders Entertainment Services Ltd/Concrete
Mr Sanders
Don
Tony
Col
Terry

Cast Cont'd

Big E's Mob
Big Elliot Williams
Frank Holms
Dennis Hilton
Liam Donahue
Kev McKay
All-Nite Shoppers' Paradise
Kumar
Man in lift/Klingon student